Breakup

Breakup

Joseph L. Piot

VANTAGE PRESS
New York

FIRST EDITION

Published by Vantage Press, Inc.
516 West 34th Street, New York, New York 10001

Manufactured in the United States of America
ISBN: 0-533-12001-2

Library of Congress Catalog Card No.: 96-90324

0 9 8 7 6 5 4 3 2 1

Introduction

Pres. R. Evans Lee sat at his massive desk in the Oval Office. So much perspiration poured from his exhausted body that the odor nauseated the normally fastidious chief executive of the United States of America. In the middle of his first term, Evans Lee was facing the disintegration of his beloved country. For more than a year the courts of the entire country had been hobbled over the separation issue. The Supreme Court had this very day authorized the issue to be placed on the November ballot. The voters would have the fate of the Union in their hands—they could vote yes or no for a constitutional change permitting states to secede.

Many things flooded the president's mind. He recalled the dilemma that must have faced his namesake, a senior Union military officer, when he resigned his allegiance to the central government to lead Confederate forces in their fight for separatism—for freedom from Washington and the right to set up their own government. Evans Lee feared the outcome of the proposed issue on a national ballot because so many people were disenchanted with the bureaucracy, the ineffectiveness, the red tape, and the high cost of central government. The president came from the South, having been raised in the climate of states' rights. He knew well that his own party had led the way to federal control over the lives of everyone in the Union. But break up the central government! Destroy more than two hundred years of progress! He had to prevent such a calamity. President Lee picked up the phone and summoned the chairman of the Joint Chiefs of Staff and the attorney general.

Breakup

Chapter One

Voter apathy had been a hazy memory for myriads of politicians. Now, they felt the ground swell of change in the air. There was a zealous desire on the part of the American electorate for massive changes in how they were governed. Town meetings began to spell out the demands of John and Mary Elector. Washington no longer represented them. The cost of central government was ridiculously expensive and what the government provided was totally ineffective. They didn't want to change just the people in Washington; they wanted a more localized government that was responsive to current issues, a governing body able to act quickly and fairly. They were disgusted with Washington and its bureaucrats. *They wanted HOME RULE!*

State house politicians, the closest link between the electorate and government, began to recognize the popular sentiment first. To them, it was at first another protest issue that would evaporate with a change in the weather. But the idea grew, and when a TV evangelist and a news commentator spoke of the changing public opinion on the same weekend, Gov. Miguel Gonzalez of California decided it was time for action. A definite outsider and new in his job, Gonzalez was not well known among the nation's governors. But—he was young and aggressive. He exuded energy and his round, happy face told people he was glad to be alive. His speeches were humorous, since he mixed

1

Spanish, Italian, French, and even Japanese words so some people thought he spoke all those languages. And he actually did.

On a Sunday afternoon in January, Mike Gonzalez went to his Sacramento office, where he had the telephone numbers of the other forty-nine governors. He phoned the residences of Bob Ho in Honolulu; Monty Edison in Springfield, Illinois; Brad Addams in Boston; and Flint Hadley in Tallahassee. To each Gonzalez explained his opinion that it would be good for them to meet and talk over the new voter sentiment. Gonzalez was surprised that each agreed to a meeting in two weeks in Palm Springs.

It was billed to the press as a golfers' holiday. In reality, Edison and Addams were delighted to escape horrible weather at home and beat the cover off the little round ball. Mostly, all five governors relaxed in a villa and talked of a new and demanding political environment.

They shared many opinions. The current problems of central government had begun more than sixty years before. The executive branch regaled in the glory of economic and military successes but lost elections when unemployment was high and business was in the doldrums. No matter who was in the White House, crime soared, cities decayed, and welfare rolls skyrocketed. Properly educating the youth became increasingly difficult. The many glories of space exploration were erased by two accidents. All good things were taken for granted. The president was responsible for anything and everything that went wrong.

The legislative branch of government, the 100 senators and 435 members of the House of Representatives, was empowered to introduce legislation, assess and collect taxes, regulate interstate and foreign commerce, establish post offices, coin money, maintain armed forces, and declare war. Besides this broad job description, Congress had cleverly devised ways of taking from those who *have* and giving to those who *want.* The more they were given, the more the recipients expected and the more often the liberals were reelected. Each new entitlement program was designed to snare yet another bloc of voters.

Addams, the crusty New Englander with piercing blue eyes and a full head of white hair that was rarely combed, thundered, "We know what the problems are! How in hell can we motivate that Washington crowd of bureaucrats when we spend every waking hour trying to stay afloat with their policies, which are aimed at destroying us?"

"I have a little sign on my desk," quipped Mike Gonzalez. " 'The marvel of history is the patience with which men and women submit to burdens unnecessarily laid upon them by their governments.' "

"Yeah, aih've heard that one. Damn true. Who said it?" asked Hadley.

"Sen. William Borah—he died in 1940, the year I was born," said Gonzalez. "Do you suppose the patience of men and women is about to run out? Here in California there are millions of people who feel they are overtaxed and underrepresented by the federal government. We are a microcosm of your states and all others, and we know there isn't a thing Washington does for us that we couldn't do much better and much less expensively for ourselves."

The other four governors nodded assent. Bob Ho, a Harvard-educated native of Hawaii of Chinese ancestry, hunched his shoulders and said, "Sure, Washington is bleeding us dry. What in hell can we do? We can't secede—what options do we have?"

"By God, Bob, why can't we secede?" asked Monty Edison, his midwestern twang exaggerated to make his point. "That's just what we ought to do! Get out of the tangled and snarled mess of Washington. Every one of our states could do a helluva lot to fund much-needed local programs with the money saved from supporting the federal government. Imagine eliminating 535 spend-happy, loose-pursed people with their hordes of lackeys. Then abolish the executive branch of federalists, who have multiplied like microbes. Shi-it, Governor Ho, you guys in Hawaii are experts at tourism—do ya think we could turn Washington into a still-bigger tourist mecca? A place where travelers of the world would visit, as they do the ruins in Rome. Show people the museums, monuments, and plenty of empty buildings. Hey, I could really get excited about such a project, and it would be an easy sell to voters in my state."

Flint Hadley, deeply tanned and trim, was nodding his head affirmatively. His southern drawl rolled out like syrup. "That's ah fantastic idea—that is, if you're ser-yous. How could we proceed? We're talking about a revolution, but we sure as hell don't want to start another civil war. Mike, you're part Mexican, aren't ya? The Mexicans know more about avoiding all-out war than anybody. Got any ideas?"

"I don't have anything specific in mind. It's only 4:45. If we start our libation period a bit early, I'd bet we could come up with some interesting thoughts."

Drinks were poured and a waiter brought in snacks. The five governors toasted each other and Brad Addams said, "Here's to breaking our citizens out of bondage."

There was a, "Hear hear," from the others, and then a long period of silence. Each was reflecting on the grave subject matter. Could they be patriots or traitors, true loyalists or fanatic revolutionaries?

Flint Hadley broke the silence. " Aih believe we ought

4

ta table the whole issuh for this evening. Maybe play some poker—you know, enjoy Mike's hospitality. Aih, for one, would feel bettah about discussing such radical action after a good night's sleep. Wouldn't it be bettah to go at it bright-eyed and bushy-tailed in the mornin'?"

Montgomery Edison grinned. "I agree on deferring till morning, but who thinks he's going to sleep tonight?"

Five governors with massive state-house problems had a pleasant evening playing cards and eating and drinking too much. As they were from totally different backgrounds and represented states with their own unique but often similar problems, it was remarkable how compatible they were. The only difference of opinion was when a time was being set for breakfast. Would it be 7:00 or 7:30?

Gonzalez promised everything would be ready at 7:15 sharp!

At minutes after seven, five men, looking like haggard tourists, staggered into the private dining area.

"Monty, you sure as hell were right on. I didn't sleep a wink. This idea is about to eat me up." It was Bob Ho talking. The others agreed.

The governors grumbled through breakfast and then headed back to their rooms to prepare for a morning constitutional and telephone calls. They were to convene at 9:00 and decide if they really had anything to talk about.

*   *   *

Edison said, "OK, Mike, you called us together. What do we do now? Any suggestions on how we might proceed?"

"Why don't we appoint someone to chair the discussions—to keep some order? Governor Addams, would you agree to do that?"

5

The true aristocrat, his crow's-feet deepened from pale blue eyes as he grinned. "Why not! If the rest of you agree. OK to use my fist as the gavel?"

"You're elected by acclamation," said his friend, Flint Hadley. "Aih think we must pledge that every single thought we discuss be confidential. When it comes time to bring othahs into the picture, it must be with the agreement of this group of five. If we decide to proceed with the thoughts of yesterday, we are going to involve certain members of our staff. Right? Aih'd be interested in your thoughts on how to maintain some sort of privacy, yeah—secrecy."

Brad Addams was deadly serious. "Every person we let in must be screened carefully—we should use the CIA procedures to check them out. My daughter is my most trusted aide, but I'm not sure how much she tells that husband of hers—have to be careful even about her. Wives are generally OK, but you young guys with one or more mistresses have to be damn careful. Let's each of us list three or four aides we feel can be trusted. Then, when we develop a plan that involves other governors we really must exercise caution. We might want to involve one or more TV evangelists and some of the more vocal and disappointed politicians. I know some in each category that would help spread the word as their own."

Addams continued, "I'm surprised that five governors are so in tune with the idea of a change. Mike, how did you select the four of us to meet with you?"

"There was no great selection process. I wanted to share ideas with strong-minded people who were not clearly dedicated to the growth of a federal government. There are others I could have invited, but that might have alerted the media."

"Ya did a good job, Mikie," said Edison in his nasal

voice. It was difficult for him to control his nervous energy. "We just got to remember that we will be in the minority. The advantage we should have—it will be to put together a grassroots program that can be developed by others."

Flint Hadley cleared his throat to get attention. "It's cleah that each of us believes in a more pure form of democracy than we have. Our central or federal gov-e-ment has grown so gigantic that it is unwieldy, and it's not likely that it can be fixed. There is no way to keep its advantages and shed the problems. We can't forget that the federal gov-e-ment isn't just in Washington—it's in virtually every city in the country—so we need to use a scalpel to remove such a malignant tumor. The president is a personal friend of mine—we served in the Senate togethah. He means well, but he will not—he cannot—do one damn thing to diminutize bureaucracy. When Monty mentioned we ought to secede I thought it was a crazy, stupid idea, but it's been on my mind all night long. We might want to considah blocs of states grouping to-gethah—it would be nice to reduce the size of state gov-e-ment as well. 'Course, in Florida about a third of our state employees are needed just to keep the feds in check—y'all probably have the same thing."

"Where do we go from here?" asked Governor Ho. "Should we each set up a task force of our most trusted people?"

"How about a think tank," Flint Hadley went on, "to come up with suggestions rathah quickly? Before we leave here in the mornin' we should agree on a list of other governors to include and the timin' of our next session. We could do the next one in Florida in a month—now that aih've warmed up to the idea, aih would like to move as quickly as possible. What do you think, Mr. Chairman?"

"Good idea! Suppose we submit a list of the staff we

7

intend to involve and the governors we think could be helpful. Hell, we know these people—we can do that before lunch. After lunch, providing Mike intends to feed us again, we can agree or disagree on the governors we invite in February. Right now, I can tell you I'd like to have the guys from Connecticut, Maine, and Vermont. I wouldn't be too happy about New York, but New Jersey . . . either way."

"Lunch is set for 12:30. Are any of you going to play golf this afternoon?" Gonzalez, the host, was asking.

"I'd love to play golf," said Monty Edison, "but this is far more important. I can wait till Florida to beat the socks off Brad."

The five state chief executives shuffled around, talking to one another and listing people to include in their brainstorming group. They discussed their fellow governors at great length, looking for knockouts rather than those to include. During lunch, a proposal was made and heartily accepted, that those present invite some of the approved governors for a personal meeting during the next few weeks.

By early afternoon, each was ready with his list. Mike Gonzalez wished to include the governors of Arizona, Washington, and Oregon. There were no objections.

Bob Ho named Alaska. No objection.

Monty Edison included Missouri, Iowa, Louisiana, Wisconsin, and Texas. No objections.

Brad Addams repeated Connecticut, Maine, and Vermont. He also wished to have New Jersey included, but he was now on the fence about New York. He could be swayed either way.

Flint Hadley named Alabama, Georgia, and both Carolinas. Then he surprised the group by including Puerto Rico. No objections.

"That would be twenty-four, counting us and if we include New York." Addams was pondering each word and retracing each state name. "They won't all come when they hear what we're talking about. Tell ya what; my opinion is we have a good list to work on. We can't be too specific when meeting with these guys; you all know that!"

Hadley interrupted. "The word is *y'all,* pronounced 'y'awl.' "

Addams laughed. "OK, Reb—y'all he'p Mr. Webster with his dictionary."

Mike Gonzalez spoke up. "I wish I felt a bit more comfortable about how to discuss these things with those I'm to meet. Can anybody help me?"

Monty Edison said, "Mike, you did a great job here. Don't change your style for the others. Let them talk about solutions to their own problems—see if they are in tune with our way of thinking. Lee Paige served in the House with me, and he'd pull Arizona out of the Union right now if he could get some backing. Have him phone me in Springfield if you wish. I'll also give you my Chicago home number if he wishes to phone me there."

Brad Addams had taken over as the whip, and he made the others feel his excitement, his zeal for the nearly insurmountable task of dismantling the federal government. "We still have a few working hours and I suggest we begin a list of some of the major items that will require deep study. For instance, we may wish to privatize the postal service, Amtrak, and federally owned power plants. What about the federal park system? This could wind up an endless agenda."

Each governor had his own suggestions. They worked through the cocktail hour right up till dinner was being served. The chief executives of five states of the federal union were on a mission. Their goal was to change the

United States from its federalistic structure to a vital and energetic new-age democracy.

During dinner, Flint Hadley mentioned his friend Eddy Domingo. Domingo was the TV evangelist with a happy face and resonant voice; his massive following was becoming more vocal politically.

"Hell, he's more to the right than Attila the Hun," said Edison. "He'd blow us out of the water in thirty minutes."

"Not so sure about that," said Gonzalez. "Reverend Eddy might be a great help to us. He's an ardent supporter of the president, but he loves and supports democracy much more. I know him. We went to different schools together. His parents live in Southern California, and he usually stops to see me when he visits them. I think he'd be an ideal guy to discuss things with."

"Maybe y'all know him better than aih do," said Hadley. "You want to call him?"

"If we agree to talk to him, we can phone him right now. He's in Newport Beach." Gonzalez surprised and also disappointed himself at how he one-upped the venerable Hadley.

Everyone agreed to speak to Domingo, and from memory Mike Gonzalez dialed the 714 area-code number. "Ed, it's Mike. You been on the water today?"

"Hi, Mike. I've been thinking about you and was going to phone you in the morning to see if we could get together. Yeah, I was out in Dad's bucket of bolts. The engine on that thing grunts and groans and the hull squeaks like crazy, but I just love it. I can be alone; no one else in his right mind would put a foot in it. Where are you—in Sacramento?"

"Ed, I'm in Palm Springs with four other governors. You know Flint Hadley." Gonzalez told him who the others were and asked if he could put all of them on the speaker phone.

Domingo greeted each of the men individually, but in his more formal and public style. He had especially kind words for the man from Florida.

"Ed," Gonzalez said, "there are no others in the room, so this call can be and is definitely off-the-record. We've been here for three days talking about how to lead a crusade to give government back to the people."

"Sounds like a very fruitful field to me. Any way I can help?"

"We'd like to talk to ya about som of our ideahs, Reverend," said Hadley. "When would be a good time to meet with ya?"

"Mike said you were breaking up in the morning. Why don't you and Mike come here? I'll pick you up at John Wayne and we can talk here at Dad's place. We'll have all the privacy we need. That would save me a trip to Sacramento—I must see Mike anyway. We half-breeds stick together, you know."

"Ed, would you like to meet some of the others?"

"I would Mike, but how could you keep it on the QT?"

"We'll be in the state plane. I'll arrange with the airport manager for you to come out to say hello. The others will then go on to LAX while Governor Hadley and I meet with you. Should I arrange for ground transportation for us?"

"I'd rather you didn't. I'll pick you up in Dad's car—it's in the same shape as his boat, but if it stops we can thumb a ride. See you at John Wayne at 8:15. Adios, amigos."

Hadley was grinning like a Cheshire cat. "Best damn ideah aih had all week. Mike, you two seem like good ole buddies. What do ya think his reaction will be?"

"Ed and I grew up together in East Los Angeles. Our

11

wives are best friends. We've been close as long as I can remember. We would do most anything to help each other personally. However, Eddy Domingo really is what he says he is on TV. If our ideas appeal to him, we can expect mountainous support. If he is against the ideas, he will fight us just as hard. Whatever, he and I will remain friends."

Bob Ho asked, "Will he leak our plans to the press or to our federalist friends?"

"We'll ask him not to. If he promises confidentially, we'll have no problem."

"Which way do you think he'll go?" asked Brad Addams.

"Seventy–thirty, our favor."

"Why? Because he's a friend of yours?"

"Because it's for the good of the people. He will understand that his people will get more for their tax money. They will have an allegiance to a more localized government—to a political structure they can see and taste. Eddy Domingo is for a justice taught by Jesus. He has empathy for all races and truly respects all people. He's much too good a man to ever be a politician."

Addams looked at Gonzalez sternly and said, "Mike, we may want to scrub this idea we've been talking about for three days and run you for president."

Gonzalez stared into space for a moment, and then his famous smile emerged. "Unfortunately, the office of presidency is now outdated. It served us well for over a hundred and fifty years. Now, for more than half a century, its major usefulness has been in wartime. I truly believe what we've been saying here the last three days—the American people have become slaves to federal bureaucracy. I hope, I believe, we are patriots dedicated to a truly democratic cause. If we are able to develop our ideas into a formidable program, I promise to dedicate my life to the reforms that government needs. I have learned more from the four of you in the last three days than from a three-year college course on political science. Inviting each of you here must have been with divine help, and I am so very thankful for your ideas and fellowship. Please, in the future, call on me anytime, any day, any night."

"You're a great host and a good idea man, Mike. I'll be calling on you often so we can build a bridge from Hawaii to California." Bob Ho shook his friend's hand warmly. Each of the other governors had warm praise and thanks for their colleagues.

Chapter Two

The State of California plane landed at the Orange County John Wayne Airport at 8:12 and taxied to the west end of the field. As soon as the plane rolled to a stop, the door was opened and the radiant face of Eddy Domingo popped inside. He greeted each man affably, hugged his friend from Florida, and then gave Mike Gonzalez a big *abrazo*.

Tears filled the evangelist's eyes as he told the governors, "Mike is my *compadre*. We are closer than any brothers I know. He probably hasn't mentioned to you that he is responsible for most of the good things in my life. He kept me out of the street gangs and he coached me through math and English. He was best man at my wedding, and today he's my number-one adviser. For all of that Miguel has accepted nothing in return. I believe he keeps Our Lord busy preparing a place for him that's equal to all he does for us down here."

"Come on, Sunday, let's get off the flowery stuff."

"Mike, I can only hope these good governors appreciate the company of one of the finest persons I've ever known. Sometimes I think you're too modest for your own good. They can only know you from your political life. Once you're out of that rat race, I hope you'll be in a position to accept the approbation for all your noble works. OK, no more on my Latino friend, who calls me Sunday, which is English for 'Domingo.' I'm anxious to hear what you've

14

been talking about—and I do expect some of your time, Mike. There are some personal issues I'm wrestling with."

Governors Ho, Edison, and Addams said their good-byes, and Eddy Domingo left with Mike Gonzalez and Flint Hadley. It was a typical Newport Beach day—bright sunshine with a temperature of seventy degrees. Governor Hadley sat in back and mentally compared the beautiful flowers lining the streets with those of Tallahassee. He had to give the planners here the nod for doing a much better job in laying out a city.

"Governor," Domingo said, "do you mind if Mike and I speak Spanish for a few minutes? It's easier for me to think in our language, and I don't get a chance to pick his brain very often."

"Please do—aih really should learn Spanish. Been thinking aih should take one of those intensive language courses, but maybe aih'm too old for that now." The governor continued to enjoy the view and gasped when he first caught sight of the ocean—it looked so much like a gigantic lake, and he now knew that's why it was called Pacific.

The Domingo family residence was a comfortable bungalow, and the guests were greeted by Roberto and Maria, the parents of Eddy. His wife and two small children were at the beach but would return to see Mike—that was certain. Even the Domingo dogs and cat were happy to see Gonzalez. Hadley was impressed by the warmth and obvious love displayed by the family.

The evangelist told his parents, in Spanish, that he and the two governors had some private matters to discuss. Mother Maria led them into the parlor, took their orders for a beverage, and left, closing the door.

Flint Hadley and Mike Gonzalez told Eddy Domingo of the conversations among the five governors and of their proposed actions. The evangelist got out of his chair and

15

paced the room. He started to speak several times, but only grunts came out.

Mother Domingo came in with a pitcher of iced tea, glasses, coffee and mugs, and a tray of pastry right out of the oven. Mike got up to help her and give her another hug and a big kiss on the cheek.

The three men sat in silence while they sampled the delectables from Maria's kitchen. Each had coffee and then the tea with fresh lemon and sprigs of mint.

"No wonder you didn't want to talk about this on the phone." Domingo was as calm as Mike had ever seen him. "I can understand how each of you must feel. I'm not so sure I see the need for such drastic measures. Why are you telling me this? Do you think I could be a party to such a movement? Do you believe I could be involved in any way?"

"Ed, we'd like your candid reaction," Mike said. "Each of us has wondered if the very thought is a seditious act—or if we have the germ of an idea that can help 260 million people better govern themselves. We need to improve the way we educate our children. It's necessary to provide increased opportunities for our families, and it's essential to aid the needy without making welfare provide an optional livelihood. Federalism has not been all that successful because its political philosophy has been to do things equally for everyone rather than do them fairly."

"I suppose both of you must head back to Capital City right away. I must think about this for more than a few minutes. Suppose I phone you, Mike. It'll take me a few days. I promise to give you my opinion, as you asked. You do understand that you will be rattling cages in every country of the world. You will be denounced by some as traitors, and by others you will be praised as innovators and saviors of democracy. I suppose you want to keep a lid on this until you are ready to go public."

16

Hadley said, "Everything must be on the QT until we know what we're going to do. Should we keep ya in the loop as we meet with othah governors?"

"I'll let you know on that. When I phone Mike, I'll give him my reaction. Hombres, this is one big pile of stuff that stinks." He flashed his infectious smile and went on, "I don't know whether to thank you for including me in or not."

The noise of children filled the Domingo house, and Mike went out to greet Ed's wife, Louisa, and their son, Roberto, and daughter, Maria. It was a happy visit, and Mike got a promise they would visit the Gonzalez family in Sacramento before returning to the East Coast. Eddy thought that a good idea so the two friends could spend some thoughtful time together.

No mention was made of their serious conversation on the drive back to the airport. The state plane had just returned from Los Angeles. Gonzalez would drop Governor Hadley off at the Los Angeles airport and then proceed to Sacramento.

Chapter Three

Gov. Bradley Addams was deluged with phone calls and a built-up list of people who wished to see him urgently. He'd been in his office for less than an hour, and he was already frustrated by the turmoil. He yelled at his executive assistant, "Get Cynthia in here!"

Cynthia Addams Spicer, the governor's daughter and chief aide, floated in, gave her father a kiss on the cheek, and asked, "Why all the fuss? Let me have those phone calls." Turning to the aide, she said, "Give me the list of people wishing to see the governor—and why. I'll then see if I can help them."

Addams grinned at his daughter, who gave the opinion that she controlled the whole goddamn world. A pretty brunette in her early forties, she could be so very diplomatic, or if it was called for, she could be as salty as a sailor. She sat across from her father and folded her hands, awaiting word from him.

"Close that damn door. I want to speak to you—alone."

The door closed, Cynthia asked, "Do I sit or stand, Governor?"

Addams laughed. "Please take care of all that crap. Also, let me know if my executive assistant is worth a shit. He gripes the hell out of me. Next—." He slumped in his chair, and for one of the few times in his life it was difficult to find the right words to say to the woman he most loved. "Dammit, I don't know how to start this—wish your mother were still with us so she could handle it. Look, sweetie, how much do you tell that guy you're sleeping with?"

"Dad! You make it sound like an illicit affair. Ben and I have been married for sixteen years, and we've given you three grandchildren."

"No matter, how much do you tell him about our business?"

"Very little, really. His legal practice doesn't depend on anything political. He is interested in how things are going, and you know how much both of us supported you in the campaign. I can't say I've ever deliberately kept anything from him—I didn't think I had reason to. Why? Have I goofed up on something?"

Brad Addams got up and came around his desk and sat next to Cynthia. "If I asked you to keep something confidential, would you? Could you, even from Ben?"

Her eyes glistened with a bit of extra moisture. "Sure, if it's important to you. I can do that."

"It's important to me . . . and . . . it's important to every American. It will take me several hours to go over things with you. Catch up on the loose ends first, and then I'll tell you about it."

"Would you rather do it at dinner? I could come over to the mansion this evening."

"Great! Call the chef and tell him what you'd like and let me know the time."

The governor started relating his story while having a predinner cocktail. He kept talking through dinner, and it was nearly 10:30 before he finished. Cynthia asked few questions, since her father was very explicit. Finally, he was able to say, "That's it, up till now."

"Dad, I suppose I should say something, but I don't know how to react. You've been in politics a very long

19

time—you obviously feel strongly about this. My reaction, I guess, is . . . I'm stunned. What are you asking me to do?"

"Think about it. Maybe take a few days off. Go to New York and see some Broadway shows. Take Ben with you, but don't tell him the issue. Just you think about it. Then, when you feel you either can or cannot support the idea, tell me."

"And?"

"If you are favorable, I'd like you to chair a 'think tank' to flush out what we should and should not do. If you have even the faintest doubt, tell me. You will still be here as my right arm—I need you more than ever."

On Tuesday afternoon, Cynthia told her father and his executive assistant that she was work weary and she'd like a few days off to see some Broadway shows. She and her husband would be gone for the rest of the week. The governor said it sounded like a good idea, since she'd been putting in too much time at the office. His concern was about the children, but she assured him the nanny would have things under control.

Montgomery Edison stayed late in his capital office. Only the security guards were still there. He dialed the residence of Gov. Luke Edward Davis in Austin and urged him to come up to see how sloppy and miserable Illinois weather could be. They agreed to meet in Chicago on Friday evening. Next, Edison phoned Dean Justice in Jefferson City. Their meeting was set for Chicago on Sunday.

Bob Ho had no trouble convincing Tim O'Donnell in Anchorage that Honolulu would be a better place to talk politics than any spot in winterized Alaska.

Gonzalez and Hadley set up discussions with neighboring chief executives to get the temper of voter feeling in their areas.

On Friday afternoon, Cynthia Spicer phoned her father in Boston. "Dad," she said, "Ben and I are having a marvelous time—but I'm personally having a serious problem about the thoughts you shared with me. I would like to discuss the matter with Ben. I believe he can not only help me in making up my mind, but he could bring up issues that would be helpful to you. What do you say, may I lay it on him?"

"You haven't mentioned anything about it to him?"

"No. I promised you I wouldn't."

"Wait a few days; then let's you and I talk about it when you get back."

"Dad, this is really deep stuff. If I don't get help from Ben, I may not have an answer for you. He knows something is bugging me."

"Maybe that's good. We'll talk about it on your return. Bye, doll."

Governor O'Donnell received a proper VIP welcome in Honolulu, and the balmy weather seemed just right for a short vacation. His wife vowed she'd spend hours working on a tan, either on the beach or beside the pool. For the governor, it would be golf, golf, golf. He also expected enough sun to talk about to the snow birds.

As Bob Ho began unfolding his story about the heavy burden of the federal government and the need for alternate solutions, O'Donnell saw his golfing time being whittled away. After all, Alaska had few taxpayers and was a heavy recipient of federal funds. The state could in no way be self-sustaining. While Governor Ho stopped short of explaining the resulting thoughts of the Palm Springs meeting, O'Donnell began to understand clearly the benefit of an amalgamation of states as suggested by Flint Hadley. Ho steered the conversation to how well their two states could work with Washington, Oregon, and Califor-

21

nia and the benefits of the North American Free Trade Agreement.

On Thursday evening, Louisa and Ed Domingo invaded the governor's mansion in Sacramento. They brought along two adorable, noisy and very curious children, ages eight and ten, to be playmates for the Gonzalez pair. The place, never quiet when the children were home, now sounded like a concert hall during a rock concert.

The governor and his pal headed for the guest house. "Me first, Mike. I need to know if you will continue to help me, not just as an adviser, but also to be a watchdog for Lou and the kids. I'm not planning to check out, but these are troubled times and anything can happen."

"I promise! I promise, and I hope you'll reciprocate."

"OK, but that won't be necessary. I'm not going to give you BS about being psychic, but amigo, I just have this uneasy feeling I mentioned to you the other day. If I'm called to answer for my deeds down here, well, I needed your assurance of help.

"Now, about you and your compatriots—I'm with you 110 percent. But there must be some early restrictions or caution signs. OK? I'd like to be at your next meeting, but I wouldn't want anyone to know about it. If that is a problem, I'd like a phone pipeline."

Governor Mike gave Ed his biggest *abrazo*. "Our meeting is over. I think I'm pleased about your decision. Let's go to the big house and protect it from the kids we spawned."

Just as they were sitting down for dinner, a phone call came on the Gonzalez private line. It was Governor Addams: "Mike, I just heard on the news that the Reverend Eddy Domingo is visiting you."

"He's in, Brad."

"Great! Have a good evening."

*   *   *

Chicago had eighteen inches of snow on the ground, the temperature was twenty degrees Fahrenheit with a twenty-five-mile-per-hour wind, and when the Texas governor stepped from his plane he knew he'd made a mistake. "This is too damn cold for Eskimos, Monty. Let's talk right here at the airport and then let me go back to Austin."

Governors Davis and Edison sought privacy in a tiny conference room in the O'Hare Terminal. Edison covered as much of the Palm Springs meeting as permitted and then let Luke Edward carry on in an anti-Washington tirade.

Finally, Davis said, "By God, Monty, ya gotta let me come to that next meetin'. No matter what! Promise that I'll be included. Those liberal bureaucrat bastards are bent on destroying this country, and I want to stop 'em."

"You're in like Flynn," Edison told him.

Governor Justice didn't like the Chicago weather either, but it didn't differ much from that of Jefferson City. He arrived at the Edison home in Northbrook in time for Sunday lunch, reminding everyone he'd gone to church before he left home.

Governor Edison was a bit concerned about how Dean Justice would react. He was a Truman-type politician and actually resembled old Harry in speech and mannerisms. After lunch, they adjourned to the cozy office Monty had set up in one of the family bedrooms. Justice listened patiently to his neighbor's story for only a few minutes before he interrupted, "Monty, I'm damned sick of hearing what Washington can and cannot do for my state. Most of those spend-happy, munificent bureaucrats have already given away the heritage of my grandchildren. It seems to me that the wise men and women we send to Congress must imbibe too heavily on Potomac water and become blithering idiots. I was hoping you had something dramatic we could talk about—something drastic like how we can get the fools out. I'm no longer interested in restricting terms. I'm really fed up and want to get every damn one of 'em out."

"Will you listen to me for a few minutes?" Governor Edison then told him about the Palm Springs meeting and as much of the discussions as authorized. "Flint Hadley is going to host the next meeting. We should have a date shortly—it's probably going to be on Sanibel Island. Interested?"

"Of course! Sure I want to be included. Are you going to level with me now? What revolutionary program did you birds come up with?"

"I've given you as much dope as I'm able. Go down there bright-eyed and . . . and . . . with an inquisitive and open mind. We might all come away from the most important event of our lives."

"Monty, you make this sound like opening the door to Armageddon."

"Could be, Dean. I'd rather believe it will open the door to a new wave of true democracy. An opportunity for all of us to continue to live in an open and expanding environment without the asphyxiating oppression of an unresponsive central government."

"OK, I think I know where you're coming from. I'm anxious to hear all the details and learn how we, in Missouri, can be a part of some new excitement. See ya in Florida."

Gov. Flint Hadley began making phone calls to the Palm Springs Five early in February suggesting the meeting be at the Saddlebrook in the Tampa Bay area in two weeks, exactly four weeks from their first meeting. Each was to tell the Florida governor who was to attend and their time of arrival. Reservations would be for the attending governor and one staff member. In Palm Springs, a decision had been made to exclude the press. Hadley told each that an important agenda item would be whether to hold a press conference at the conclusion of the meetings on Wednesday morning. He also told them evangelist Eddy Domingo would be in attendance as a guest.

Brad Addams had not given his daughter permission to discuss matters with Ben. He called her into his office and asked, "Have you mentioned anything to Ben?"

"Of course not! You were to discuss it with me when we returned, and I'm still waiting for your approval." She was testy and didn't have the usual lilt in her voice.

"Suppose you and Ben have lunch with me. It would be great if you could make it today."

Cynthia walked out of his office without saying a word. An hour later, the governor's secretary told him Mr. and Mrs. Spicer would join him for lunch.

"Good. Please arrange for some sandwiches and whatever beverages they'd like. Coffee for me."

Ben Spicer entered the executive office smiling. "Hi, Governor. You're looking good, but I wish your disposition were better. My wife has been tied in knots for a week, and I know damn well it's because of you. I've deferred an important meeting to come over here—so I'm not in the mood to listen to anyone pontificate. I—"

The governor interrupted, "Let's grab some lunch and we can talk. Anyway, Ben, I plead guilty to your charges and I understand your attitude."

Nibbling on a sandwich, Addams told his daughter and son-in-law of the need for secrecy and that he may have been testing Cynthia's ability at confidentiality among others rather than from Ben. Both looked at him in disbelief.

"Dad, that's hokum and you know it. I accept the need for secrecy, but I don't appreciate not being trusted."

"Guess I screwed up. I apologize. Ben, what happened is I discussed with Cynthia a very radical political move and asked her to think about it and tell me if she could support the program. She phoned me from New York to say she needed to discuss the matter with you before she could given an answer. I put her off."

"You two are too damn close, you know that. Tell her, tell me what you want either of us to do so we don't have a father-daughter squabble," Ben said.

"Cynthia, will you give Ben the whole load? I'd like to listen in so I can be sure I told you everything."

"How long will this take?" Ben asked.

"At least an hour—maybe even two," his wife told him.

"Let me make a few phone calls so we can get on with it."

Cynthia Addams Spicer spoke like a robot. She covered every single point the governor had made and raised some ideas of her own. It took her one hour and twenty-five minutes. When she concluded, she was weary but thankful her husband knew what was eating her. She told Ben she had been asked to chair a think tank if she could support the ideas.

Brad Addams got out of his chair and said he'd take a walk. "Be back in about thirty minutes—that OK?"

Both nodded affirmatively and Addams closed the door on his way out. It was nearly an hour before he returned.

"What do you think?" The governor looked at Ben Spicer.

"It's radical, as you said. Seems like a damn good idea

26

to me, and I think you'll get widespread support. It's really an exciting concept, Brad. Cynthia and I have been talking about the pros and cons of her involvement. What she decides to do is up to her, and I will support her decision. The liberals, the conservatives, the press, they all are going to try to burn your ass, you know that."

"I know that! Kiddo, are you in or out?"

"I'll give you my answer before I leave this evening."

*   *   *

His brief visit and conversation with Monty Edison continuously nagged Luke Edward Davis. As governor of the great state of Texas, he was entitled to more information—and, by God, he'd get it.

Phoning Tallahassee, he said, "Hello, Flint, this is Luke Edward." The friends spoke of family, health, and aging until Davis was near the boiling point. "Flint, I visited Monty Edison a few days ago to talk about some mutual problems. He told me of a meetin' y'all had in Palm Springs and said one was planned in Florida. The rascal skirted around specific points so much that aih'm wound up real tight. What the hell's goin' on?"

"Luke Edward, Monty probably gave you the information he was authorized to pass on. Aih can tell ya we were discussin' drastic measures to solve some of our political, social, and economic problems. Y'all come to our next meetin' for full details. Our thoughts are under wraps because our proposals are from far out in right field."

"Hey, man, what the hell'er ya talkin' bout? Secedin' from the goddamn Union?"

"Now, mah good buddy, aih'm not gonna violate mah promise of confidentiality. Since the meetin's heah in Florida, y'all might want to bring one or more of your

27

special politicos. How 'bout Herb Fullman? Ya still on good terms with him?"

"Course. Herbie's been restin' up after gettin' his ass whipped by Evans Lee in his run for the presidency. He's thinkin' he may run for the Senate again. How 'bout our ex-president? Clay Farrington is itchin' to get a bit in his mouth."

"Jeez, Luke Edward, aih don't know 'bout him. Guess aih better tell ya our plans would do away with Congress."

"Great! Flint, that's fantastic! Aih promise to tell him only what Monty told me. Hot damn, are we gonna have fun at your place! Be back in touch in a day or two."

Flint Hadley immediately relayed the conversation to Governors Addams, Edison, Ho, and Martinez. None objected to an invitation to such prominent statesmen.

Chapter Four

On the third Sunday in February much of the North and East of the United States was under a winter siege. It was freezing in Phoenix, and ice covered Dallas. At the Saddlebrook, a lazy breeze spread the seventy-degree temperature evenly over the gardens, the golf course, and the tennis courts. Everyone had to agree that this was a wonderful place to—well, to do anything that needed to be done.

The evening reception was a "get acquainted" session. The small talk indicated everyone was interested in more value for their tax dollars, but if a poll were taken about the need for a central government, the federalists would win going away.

New York's governor, Emmett Brown, asked Rev. Eddy Domingo in a voice loud enough to turn heads, "Reverend, are you preparing to bring your TV malarkey to the political arena?"

Domingo flashed his brightest smile and said in a very moderate tone, "Governor, I'm here to learn about the problems of our people from those of you who should be the experts. If I can encourage just one politician to be less political and more concerned about people issues, I'll feel my time is well spent."

"I've heard of your TV show, Reverend. Ain't you with those other right wingers like Falwell and Robertson?"

"Governor, I'm flattered that you put me in the category with such prominent evangelists. They are both great patriots and they do a wonderful job of bringing the Word of God to us. Tell me what you mean by 'TV malarkey,' Governor Brown. I'm always anxious to improve, and I'd be grateful for your advice."

Brown had drawn in many listeners, and he was now embarrassed. His tone lowered considerably as he said, "I believe I used the wrong word, Reverend. What I meant to say was that you preach to large crowds and the television audience eats up what you say. You could persuade many voters if you chose to enter politics."

There was a ringing bell that called everyone to attention. Gov. Flint Hadley offered an official welcome and told them "Activity Schedules" were being delivered to their rooms. He said, "Just in case y'all 'er too pooped to read it tonight, I'll tell ya there will be a plenary session at 9:30 Monday mornin'. No members of the media will be present for any of the sessions on Monday or Tuesday. We have tentatively arranged a news conference on Wednesday mornin' at 11:30, but y'all will have an opportunity to alter that. The hotel staff has arranged a variety of activities for wives and husbands not in the meetin's. Please enjoy our Florida hospitality—and thank y'all for comin'."

Governor Addams chaired the opening session, and without saying so, he followed the pattern of the Palm Springs meeting. Within minutes, a heated discussion unfolded about a much more demanding electorate and the inability of states to cope with their needs.

At the end of an hour, a fifteen-minute break was scheduled. Governor Addams suggested that on their reconvening, they break up into eight groups of six. "You governors can determine if you wish your aide in your group. After lunch, we'll send our trusted advisers to another room to start their own brainstorming sessions."

Addams and Hadley spoke briefly. Hadley said, "Aih'm sure as hell surprised that every single one on our list came. Aih wonder what impact Clay Farrington and Herb Fullman will have? Think they might present a logical negative point of view? Could be good, huh? Aih hope we get a good airing of the issuhs and determine if this is a viable course of action."

Addams thought for a moment, then commented, "Both are brilliant men with loads of experience and a massive following. Agree with us on a confederation of new states? I've no idea, but their opposing points of view may help us sharpen our own issues. Before this day is over we should know what we are fighting for and what we are fighting against. Don't you agree?"

Flint replied, "Yeah, aih sure do. Aih'm afraid we'll need a committee to call the president and tell him what we've talked about before that news conference. It will break his heart—it does mine—but aih'm becoming convinced there is no better way. What was the flack Emmett was raisin' with Eddy Domingo?"

"Nothing much. Brown likes to intimidate people if he can. Domingo proved much too smooth for him. I hope the reverend will support whatever program comes out of here. He could ignite people like crazy."

Eight groups of six around tables in a single room may not have been a wise choice. One could hear testy voices trying to gain enough volume to be in command, but that wasn't working at all.

Cynthia Spicer was with Governors Brown of New York, Davis of Texas, Justice of Missouri, and Farris of Virginia. The sixth member was Bob Smith, the aide to Clive Roberts of New Jersey. Mrs. Spicer didn't take long to establish herself as an authority on state government and its problems. She cleverly guided Brown and Farris into the thought pattern set out by her father.

Luke Edward Davis needed no help. He was vocal and his comments were strategic—his criticism of the federal government ended in the remark, "Why do we need those bureaucrats to tell us how to run our states? Very few of them know our problems firsthand, and not one is as concerned about your state or mine as they are about being reelected."

Cynthia led him into the next step when she asked, "What should the states do, Governor?"

"By God, lovely lady, my state, all the states, should secede! Washington is attempting to run our lives—instead, they are ruining our lives."

No one at the table seemed shocked. They were all uncharacteristically quiet. Brown broke the silence, "Luke Edward, I guess I'm startled to hear that. I surely would never have considered such an action . . . but . . . it sounds like a viable solution to some of our problems . . . but it's wild and troublesome to me. I guess I'd like to hear how that could be played out. Doesn't seem like a good idea to have fifty new countries applying for membership in the United Nations."

Dean Justice shuffled in his chair. "Harry Truman might be rolling over in his grave, but I'll bet he'd be supporting this idea to the hilt. We could group enough states together to be commercially effective and yet keep the areas small enough for the electorate to be much better served."

Rodney Farris, the Virginian, had been deep in thought. A brilliant lawyer and one of the outstanding black politicians in the country, he commented, "I guess I'm with Emmett in that I'd like to hear how such action might work. It's obvious from this table that it's not another North versus South, but holy God, how can we proceed?"

Bob Smith, the New Jersey governor's aide, was almost afraid to comment. "I suppose it will be up to us, Mrs. Spicer, and the other aides to develop strategic plans. First I'd like to discuss the matter with Governor Roberts."

"Tell him how we feel. This would be a wonderful chance for New York and New Jersey to finally get together." Emmett Brown sat back in his chair and was more relaxed than he'd been since moving into the Albany state house.

It was time for lunch. Chairman Addams proposed they take an hour and a half so that conversations could be continued at the tables. "After lunch, our advisers will adjourn to the adjacent meeting room. We won't give them an agenda—let them develop things on their own. After all, they are much smarter than we governors."

Eddy Domingo added, "And the evangelist."

*   *   *

The aides to Domingo and the Palm Springs Five had met earlier in the morning and decided to spread themselves out so they might guide any of those who got stuck. They would propose six groups of four and try to encourage everyone to be innovative.

The schedule called for the afternoon session to run from 1:30 until 5:30, with no assigned break time. Then, a cocktail party from 7:00 till 7:45, with dinner at 8:00.

Only a few thirsty people showed up for the cocktail party; nearly all the tables of four worked until 7:30. The governors rehashed many times the issues that had led them to talk about a new democracy. They questioned how they could govern without a central authority. Was it reasonable to divide into fifty new governments? How would disputes between states be handled? Whose picture would be on the currency? And even more seriously, how could they resolve the issues of crime, decaying cities, exorbitant taxes, and entitlement programs? Some were on the fence, but not a single one felt strongly against eliminating the Washington bureaucracy as well as the hierarchy.

When the people gathered for dinner, it was a somber crowd. Cynthia told her father there was enthusiasm and apprehension. When asked if they needed some direction, she smiled and told him they could do quite well on their own.

Governor Addams told the dinner assembly he and Governor Hadley were being pressured by the media, who arrogantly insisted on knowing why so many heads of states were assembled. He told them it was a winter's golf holiday and suggested that all the golfers be out on the courses in the morning.

"Besides," he told them, "our advisers seem to be making some remarkable headway, and it's just possible they might have a report ready for us after lunch tomorrow. I guess what I'm telling you is to meet again after dinner if you have anything to get off your chests and relax in the morning."

They all seemed to race through dinner, after which the governors and their aides conferred well into the night.

The second plenary meeting started immediately after lunch on Tuesday. Governor Addams called the dignified group to order and asked if any of the governors had questions—or a statement. Everyone was unusually quiet until the Texas governor, Luke Edwards Davis, went to a microphone. "Aih'm not sure I want to hear what these good people will have to say. They were given the Herculean task of taking our ideas and putting them into some rational order. Some of us, governors and advisers, were still meetin' at 3:00 A.M. You and aih are in favor of a movement that disturbs me. Aih never dreamed aih could support such action—aih can't even say the word. Mr. Chairman. I'd like to suggest that we governors meet alone after we hear the advisers' report. Reverend Domingo, I hope you will join us. We need some prayerful advice and . . . and God's help."

The advisory group had chosen Randall Berger of New York as its chairman. He began, "We followed your instructions and added ideas of our own. There is no way to lessen the impact of what our report says. Possibly this is only a discussion or starting point. What we have on paper will surely require many revisions, but of the twenty-four of us, there is not a single person objecting. It took us only minutes to recognize that Cynthia Addams Spicer is the outstanding parliamentarian among us, and we've asked her to present the key points of our report to you."

When Cynthia stepped to the podium, her father was tremendously proud, but there was an ache in his heart that her mother couldn't see and hear their marvelous, intelligent, beautiful daughter.

She began, "Mr. President, governors, ladies and gentlemen, a final document may be months away, so we have skipped the *wherefore, whereas,* and other formal legal terminology. Rather, we'll give you bulleted points and highlights. Please interrupt immediately when you have comments or questions. Each of your advisers has a statement copy in a code he or she understands. This is to help preserve confidentiality until after your news conference tomorrow. Also, I believe some of you wish to discuss certain issues with President Lee before meeting with the press.

"I've been cautioned to soften the main thrust of this meeting or else some of you will go white-haired as we speak. I'm sorry; there is no way to back into this issue.

"The states represented here should have the right to secede from the federal union.

"The time period should be within six months.

"Only twenty-four states are represented at this meeting. The other twenty-six states are to be contacted within the next thirty days to offer their points of view.

"In addition to the Commonwealth of Puerto Rico, it is felt certain areas of Canada and Mexico should be kept apprised of our actions.

"Considering that a majority of the other states may be willing to join this coalition, it is proposed that a confederation of eight American states be formed. This is to be done by the grouping of current adjacent sovereign areas."

Gov. Edward Sebastian of South Carolina interrupted, "Mrs. Addams Spicer, can you help me out? Please explain what your committee is proposin', say, for my state."

Cynthia was pleased for the break. It gave her time for a sip of water and to settle down a little. "Governor, we've been so bold as to name the new country/states—South Carolina would be in South Atlantica, and the other members would be North Carolina, Georgia, Florida, Alabama, and—hold your hat—Puerto Rico and Cuba."

"I'll be damned; I like that. I really like that!"

The room burst into applause.

Governor Brown said, "Madam, you've piqued my curiosity. What about my state?"

"Governor, the proposal is for Colombia to include Michigan, Indiana, Ohio, Pennsylvania, and western New

York. In New England there would be Maine, Vermont, New Hampshire, Massachusetts, Connecticut, eastern New York, New Jersey, Delaware, and New Brunswick."

"Somebody has a very innovative mind. The thought of dividing up New York took a lot of thought—it just might be a good idea, a really good idea." Brown was not at all offended.

"Miz Cynthia," Reverend Domingo asked, "I believe all the governors here are curious about the suggested confederation members. Could you please tell us the others?"

"Certainly: we recognize that this may go through repeated revisions. Here is our present proposal: Pacifica will be composed of Washington State, Oregon, California, Hawaii, Alaska, Nevada, and Arizona. It might also include Baja California and British Columbia, should they request membership.

"The Rocky Mountain Empire would be Montana, Idaho, Wyoming, Colorado, Utah, New Mexico, and the possibility of Sonora, Mexico.

"The American Heartland will be North Dakota, South Dakota, western Minnesota, Nebraska, Kansas, Oklahoma, Texas, and, again possibly, Nuevo León.

"Mississippi will be eastern Minnesota, Wisconsin, Iowa, Missouri, Illinois, Arkansas, Kentucky, Tennessee, Louisiana, and Mississippi.

"The eighth country/state will be North Atlantica, composed of Virginia, West Virginia, District of Columbia, Maryland, and Rhode Island.

"Your advisers felt this list would become a negotiating item as details for the confederation are developed. What is your opinion, ladies and gentlemen?"

To a man and woman, they stood up, and the applause was loud and long.

When they sat down, Governor Hadley asked, "Cynthia, what is the first thorn in the hedgerow?"

"We feel it important that a representative group of governors phone the president this evening or no later than tomorrow morning and explain the developments of this meeting."

"Right you are. Your daddy and aih agree. We need several more who know the president well. Who wishes to be included?"

Govs. Betty Davies of Vermont, Davis of Texas, Brown of New York, and Roberts of New Jersey raised their hands, as did former president Farrington and ex-senator Fullman.

Flint Hadley stood and smiled like a Cheshire cat. "Thank ya, that's a task none of us relish." He looked at the former president and continued, "We should discuss how to tell Evans Lee what he may already know."

Many of the council members were squirming in their seats, and Randall Berger rapped for order. "We have many more things for you to consider. Cynthia, will you carry on, please."

The gracious lady, who would have been beautiful except for the rather large English nose inherited from her father, stepped back to the podium. "There is hardly any specific order in what we propose. As you just did, please interrupt at any time. Your comments or questions will give us future guidance. The following are again for your consideration.

"The confederation will continue the use of the dollar as its standard of currency. Its valuation and support will be determined when the makeup of the states is finally resolved. Of course a new design will be required, but we don't expect a hassle over whose picture adorns it, do we?

"There will be no tariffs, duties or import-export regulations among the eight states.

"Each of the eight will apply to the UN for separate membership.

"Educational standards are to be set by the various states. Programs for superior learners should be a part of each system. The education of our young people must be a priority for every state of the confederation.

"We suggest the eight minimize government influence."

Gov. Diana Bloom of Ohio asked, "What do you mean by that?"

Spicer replied, "Fewer bureaucrats. If this is to be a successful revolution, it must cede a new patriotism to local governments instead of to Washington or even to the new capitals of the confederation. I suppose the concern is that all the federal, state, and local government personnel might be reassigned within the new confederation."

There was a round of applause and shouts of, "Hear, hear!"

"Each country/state will set up its own tax base.

"We have not yet developed an effective way of deemphasizing Washington, D.C. It will become a part of North Atlantica. One thought is for Washington to house a court of arbitration, one jurist appointed from each state and a ninth to be elected as chief arbitrator. All federal offices will be abolished as well as Congress (535 men and women and their staffs). Federal offices outside the District will be abolished and their activities assumed by the states."

Sporting an impish grin, Cynthia offered, "Washington, D.C., will be reduced to a major tourist attraction featuring its beautiful monuments and wonderful museums and cavernous empty buildings."

Uproarious laughter filled the room, then strong applause.

"Your advisory group believes that there should be a massive effort to privatize federal activities such as the Postal Service, Amtrak, and the Power Authorities. Current federal agencies will all be abolished, saving many billions of dollars each year. You, the states, will assume only those you deem worthwhile."

Near-pandemonium broke out with hooting and whistling—the bedlam rivaled the college roar of a home-team touchdown.

"The eight will have new and added responsibilities. You will have a renewed and larger tax base that must be spent wisely. Here are some thoughts:

"Each new state will pick up its share of entitlement programs. Social Security, health care, federal government, and military retirement costs and welfare programs. The costs the eight are to assume will be based upon population.

"Foreign aid will be decided upon by the confederation group. No detailed suggestions have yet been worked out.

"The new states are to assume control of the highways, bridges, and dams within their jurisdiction and to provide funding for maintenance and expansion.

"Most subsidy programs are to be eliminated.

"There should be some shared universal programs—such as space and certain medical and research centers.

"We've time for only two more points. The first may be one of the thorniest.

"The eight are not to be policemen to the world. Military bases and the military complex that now spread from the Pentagon to locations completely around the world should not be fractionalized. Foreign bases ought to

40

be closed rather quickly. Each state will decide on the continuation of bases within its territory, and they could be part of a unified organization.

"Your advisers recommend that there be a single central government in each of the eight states. This follows our theme of reducing the number of bureaucrats.

"Your team of advisers recognizes it has just scratched the surface of reasonable changes that could and should be made. There is still much work to be done."

There was generous and lengthy applause. Governor Addams rapped the group to order and said, "We have a remarkably talented group of advisers. Each of us should individually and then collectively study these recommendations. They sound so practical that something must be wrong with them. If they are so reasonable, why haven't we done these things before? Let's ask ourselves all the hard questions before we meet with the press tomorrow morning. Those of us who are to speak to the president should meet in one hour. All of you are invited to participate—we hope we are on the road to a true democracy within a confederation of states, each of which will be a republic."

Governor Addams continued, "We are honored to have with us two of our country's most revered political leaders. I'm surprised they've been quiet for so long. We must have a few words from each of them now. The Honorable Herbert Fullman spent sixteen years in the United States Senate and two years ago he made a strong run for the presidency. Most of us know him as an advocate for a lower-cost government and an end to many of the onerous entitlements. Please say 'hello' to Sen. Herb Fullman."

Herbert Fullman stood to his full six feet, five inches and moved to the podium. "It's nice to be with you. Coming from Pittsburgh at this time of year, it's nice to be most anyplace else. I must commend my friend Flint Hadley for turning on fabulous weather and all of you for making me feel comfortable. I arrived Sunday afternoon, and I've tried to stay out of your way rather than interfere with the processes.

"While some of you were playing golf this morning, I visited with the advisory teams that put together the report you just heard. I had an opportunity to discuss issues with team members, and I'm impressed at the quality of the work they've done.

"What you seem to be thinking about, breaking up the federal union, is a thought-provoking and very serious matter. Is it possible? Is it workable? Do I support your majority view? I don't know. The idea clouds my mind so thoroughly that I'm not able to think things through. Am I impressed? Do I wish to hear more? Yes! I say yes because I've listened to so many points that deserve to be heard by the governing men and women of this country that it would be criminal for them to be suppressed. With your permission, I'd like to continue my role, almost as a student of political philosophy, for the remainder of your meetings." The senator was generously applauded.

Governor Addams spoke again. "For seven years, this next man was the occupant of the Oval Office. He served government for more years than many of you can count birthdays. When I was first in the Senate, he was the man who put fire in the belly of the troops. Some called him Clay Brimstone. I don't need to give a flowery introduction, because Clayton Farrington built a rock-solid and enviable reputation. We admire him, we respect him, but, more important, we love him. Yes, Mr. President, we love you."

There was standing applause as the former president stepped to the microphone. "Thank you, Brad. Ladies and gentlemen, it's nice to be with so many friends in this day and age, when politicians have so few friends. Those of you who have known me for a long time know Brad Addams was speaking the truth when he said I was Ole Brimstone. However, you should know Brad hasn't always been the patrician gentleman. I spoke to Cynthia and Ben Spicer and learned he's mellowed considerably, except to his daughter and son-in-law.

"Many of us go back a long way in government. We've shared the barbs and prefer to remember mostly the good things. Flint Hadley, Luke Edward Davis, and I were having a little libation before dinner and I asked if I'd be expected to endorse your ideas and say t' at all of you are wonderful people. Luke Edward said, 'Hell no, no one would believe that 'cause most of us know you are a miserable, cantankerous SOB.'

"So I can only tell you how I feel. You are treading on the edge of sacred ground in governmental history. You may be right—you may be dead wrong. Continue to study both sides of your program. Explore every option.

"There are many things our government doesn't do very well. One of them is run businesses—like TVA, Amtrak, even the postal system.

"This afternoon, Randall Berger, Bob Smith, and Cynthia Spicer were sharing with me their thoughts on ways to fight crime and clean up our cities. When their ideas are jelled, listen to them. Even if you leave Tampa and forget what you've been talking about here, you must implement some of their suggestions.

"I suppose I should be asking a key question, even if it's much too late, like 'where in the hell were all of you with these great ideas when I was pleading for help from 1600 Pennsylvania Avenue?' "

The former president had tears in his eyes. "You have some very fertile minds at work. Study every option very carefully, since your decisions could have an enormous impact on the future of America."

There was a great hush; then everyone rose to give Clay Farrington the recognition he richly deserved.

The conference room filled with governors and guests who wished to be included in the conversation with the president. Flint Hadley summoned help from the Saddlebrook staff. They needed telephone attachments so any one of two dozen men and women could hear and speak. The hotel supplied their needs in minutes. Governor Hadley then asked Reverend Domingo if he would lead them in prayer before they settled on the "what" and "how to" of a difficult conversation.

Eddy Domingo bowed his head and then in his melodious voice said, "Father in heaven, we come to you as men and women of many creeds and different races. Each of us is shouldering a grave responsibility because we love your sons and daughters so very much. They are also our people, Lord, and we ask you to help us do what is right for every one of them, from the just-conceived to the very aged. Guide us in our conversation with the president of the United States, a good man and one of your true servants. We must tell him that now is the time to make changes in the way our people are governed. We wish him to know we are patriots dedicated to a noble cause. With your help, Father, we will love and serve you better."

A great quiet spread over the room. Someone coughed and Governor Addams said, "Flint Hadley and I spoke of this telephone call earlier. It's not something either of us relishes, but we owe it to the president. Any suggestions on how it should be played out?"

"Governor, why don't you and Flint make the call, tell the president we've been meeting for three days, and wing

44

it?" It was Mike Gonzalez speaking, "With your permission, anyone here can say his or her piece. That way it won't sound as if we have a well-rehearsed story to tell him—since we don't."

"Sounds like a good idea to me," said Donna Jensen. "Why don't we make the call right now without further discussion? Every one of us has an individual opinion that could help President Lee understand our point of view. We can't possibly expect him to agree with us. Isn't the call a matter of courtesy before we go public?"

When Brad Addams asked if there were other points of view, the group was silent. "OK, let's dial the man!"

Chapter Five

Addams identified himself, saying he wished to speak to the president. Art Butler, the White House chief of staff, had answered the phone. He and Addams bantered for a few moments, and then Butler reluctantly switched the call directly to the president.

President Lee came on the phone saying, "Hello, Brad. I understand you and some of your friends have been having a very secretive meeting. Want to tell me about it?"

"Mr. President, as I told Art, we have twenty-four governors, Eddy Domingo, and some other interested people wired into the phone service so we can tell you what we've been talking about before we have a press conference in the morning."

"Mr. President, Flint Hadley heah."

"With you there, Flint, I can be assured there have been plenty of sparks flying."

"Not really, Evans. Our discussions have been the most serious in mah lifetime, maybe the most critical evah in this country. Aih'm certain that not all people here think alike, but aih'm confident their goals are the same."

"OK, Flint. What the hell have you been talking about that's so secretive and momentous?"

"Mr. President, this is Betty Davies."

"Hi, Princess; I'm delighted to hear your voice."

"Mr. President, a few minutes ago when we started speaking about this call to you, Reverend Domingo gave an invocation. Since I'll never forget having been a secretary, I took it down in shorthand. I'd like for you to hear what he said." She then read Domingo's words before anyone could comment.

"Hello, Eddy," the president said. "You know you're among some of the best people in the country. I hope you've all had a wonderful time at that beautiful place. I've been a privileged guest of Flint Hadley at the Saddlebrook on several occasions. It must be great to be there on the golf course while we're freezing our tails off in Washington."

"No golfing, Mr. President. This is Emmett Brown. We've had very serious discussions about how to best represent our constituents. You are well aware of the groundswell among voters claiming they are overtaxed and underrepresented by the federal government."

"Emmett, these are tough times; you know that. You also know the Congress ties my hands every time I want to do something for the people."

Flint Hadley held up his hands indicating he was ready to tell the president what they had on their minds. "Mr. President, we've been—"

"What in the hell's wrong, Flint? You and I have been on a first-name basis for more than forty years."

"Evans, we've been meetin' now for two and a half days. Those here represent both major parties, and there are several independents. We have cussed and discussed every issuh of state and federal government. We are of the opinion and we will make a statement to the media in the mornin' that our states have the right to secede from the federal government. Federalism is no longer workin' and we must explore alternate ways."

"Flint! Are you talking about starting a second civil war?"

"Certainly not, Evans. This is the most peace-lovin',

dedicated group of men and women aih've ever met. We just recognize that the bureaucracy of the central government is not workin'. It is stifling everyone and everything and remedial action is demanded."

"Governors! That's sedition. Do you all wish to be branded as traitors?"

"Mr. President—Brad Addams. You know full well that the federal government is not working well. We respect you for your intelligence and integrity, but neither you nor anyone else in the Oval Office could fix the problems of the federal government. It's gotten out of hand. It is absolutely essential that we try a more democratic form of government while we are still able to call ourselves a republic."

"Brad, this is one helluva shock. You understand that I am commander in chief of the armed forces and would be obliged to use the military to prevent any seditious act."

"Mr. President, we are only in the formative stages of a plan. We will keep you abreast of our ideas. I assure you we are not going to cause the need to have all the cannons unmuzzled. I am embarrassed by our proposed solutions and yet pleased at the patriotism of this group. Not a single one is thinking of his or her own state, but rather the welfare of our people."

"And you're not willing to give me an opportunity to fix what's wrong?"

Hadley was speaking again. "Evans, the cost of the executive branch is out of reason. There are 535 spendthrift members of Congress that each cost us much more than a million a year. If you and aih were to sit down and talk this over, you would agree with what we would like to do."

"Can you defer that press conference?"

"No, sir, aih don't think that would be wise. We will

try to sanitize it as much as possible. Aih can phone you the moment it concludes."

"Do that, Flint. Also, how about you, Brad, and Mike Gonzalez coming to see me? You certainly don't want to destroy two hundred years of progress. To all of you, my thanks for being candid. I know you are hurting. I know our people are hurting more. Let's see if we can work things out."

Phones were hung up. Thirty men and women were limp with fatigue. They spoke in quiet tones of the president's reaction and wondered how best to handle the press conference. Their advisers were called in for their expert opinions.

At 11:30 Wednesday morning, the press conference began. "I am Randall Berger, chairman of the governors' advisory committee. We will have a statement and then give you an opportunity to ask questions."

"Do you have written minutes of your meeting for us?" asked a reporter.

"No," replied Berger. "Mrs. Cynthia Spicer, aide to Governor Addams, will give the statement, and you will see that she has no prepared notes."

Spicer began. "Twenty-four governors, including Governor Fuentes of Puerto Rico, have been meeting for nearly three days. Also involved were Rev. Eddy Domingo and a single aide for each. Additionally, several other guests have been present."

"Will you give us a list of the attending governors?" asked a *New York Times* reporter.

Berger said, "When Mrs. Spicer has finished her statement, we will take questions."

Spicer continued, "Discussions centered on a single topic—how to better respond to the wishes and the needs of the American people. It is the opinion of those who have been in the discussions that the federal government has lost its ability to serve the electorate. Washington no longer adequately represents voters. There is a feeling the cost of the central government is ridiculously expensive and totally ineffective.

"Items of discussion have included: the ballooning bureaucracy population, unwieldy aspects of the gigantic federal government, duplication of efforts by the states, inequitable entitlement programs, welfare as a livelihood, as a profession, and businesses the federal government should not be in.

"The advisory committee has generated potential solutions to some of these issues. More options need to be generated before we are ready to suggest specific solutions. Though myriads of answers are being sought, many here feel a referendum might be in order to change our political status."

Mrs. Spicer stepped back from the podium, and Berger stepped up to say they would take questions.

"Are you talking about secession?" The question came from the front row.

Berger was extremely calm; "Please state your name and affiliation when asking questions. First, I'd like to introduce those governors who are ready to answer your questions." He then asked Governors Brown, Gonzalez, Edison, Addams, Hadley, and Jensen to step forward. "You may direct your questions to a particular person or to the governors as a group."

"Marty Benton, *New York Times.* Are you talking about secession?"

Governor Hadley stepped to the microphone. "Our discussions have been focused on the plight of the taxpayers, the private citizens and the people who have been devastated by big government. We are searchin' for an alternative that will solve fiscal problems and yet be cognizant of people problems. We are probably a long way from making specific proposals that would require a national referendum."

"Then secession is under consideration?" It was Benton again.

Hadley replied, "Our goal is to improve our current political process. Many options are being considered." Turning to the other governors, he asked, "Can any of you expand on my reply?" Each shook their head.

"Helen Reed, *Washington Post.* I understand you spoke to the president last evening. Will you tell us what the discussion was about?"

Governor Hadley stepped to the microphone again. "The president and aih have been close friends for more than forty years, and the call to him was to tune him in to our thoughts. The discussion was private. Any comments would have to come from President Lee directly or at least from the White House."

"Betty Halpert, CNN. Is there any particular reason your meetings have been so secretive? And a follow-up question—do you have an agenda for telling your fellow governors what's gone on here?"

Governor Addams responded, "Our discussions have been an exploration of ideas. We will be in contact with each of the other governors within a very short time. I know it's of concern to some of you that we do not have a handout that is The Saddlebrook Manifesto, so to speak. The moment we start putting things on paper there is a tendency to consider the ideas as cast in stone. We intend to keep our thoughts fluid until our objectives develop into a pattern. Just as soon as we've developed a series of appropriate options, we'll tell you about them. On your follow-up, Ms. Halpert, we certainly will be in touch with our fellow state administrators. We believe they will be able to help us zero in on various choices."

"Tim Mafew, *Manchester Guardian.* You are giving evasive answers, aren't you, Governor?"

Governor Gonzalez replied, "I can understand how you might feel that way. Please understand that we have been sharing a multitude of ideas and we cannot let anyone render decisions on them before the other governors have an opportunity for their analyses. The American media has reasonably reported voter discontent. We are searching for solutions."

"Ryan, NBC. Can't we help?" There was general laughter.

Gonzalez said, "Miss Ryan, we are open to advice from everyone. I have great respect for the media and its ability to apprise the public of what is happening. In just a few days we've generated so many different concepts for governmental change that we now must take time to distill our thoughts. Can you help? Surely, just as soon as we can jell some specific suggestions."

"Meeker, Reuters. Is it significant that you have an ethnic, racial, and gender mix to answer our questions?"

Governor Donna Jensen came to the mike and gave the group her engaging smile and in her unique Wisconsin accent said, "I hope so; we're all governors. I might add to some of the comments made by my fellow executives that I am particularly anxious to share the ideas of this meeting with those governors who are not here."

"Ready, CBS. Who selected the people to attend this meeting?"

Governor Hadley scratched his head and said, "There wasn't such a thing as a selection committee. In discussions with one anothah, we included those we had an opportunity to speak to. No one was left out for any reason.

Can someone else help me out? Why do we have so many or so few governors heah? And why are we the ones heah rather than othahs?"

Governor Edison said, "I think you have it right, Flint. During our conversations it seemed important to meet rather quickly and explore potentials that could be helpful to all our people. Course there's another reason for some of us who are snow birds—this has been a rough winter."

Benton asked, "Why was Reverend Domingo included? Could it be that you wish him to lead a third party?"

Edison said, "Reverend Domingo, why don't you answer that question?"

There was a hall of camera flashes when Eddy Domingo came to the rostrum. He paused only long enough for things to settle down. "I am a minister of the Gospel—I am not, and could not be, a politician. Two of my close friends are governors. Another special friend is the president of the United States. I regularly speak with Governor Gonzalez. We were raised together and he's been my adviser and pal since high school. Governor Mike and I are *compadres,* closer than most brothers. Governor Hadley and I have shared the same concerns for people since I first met him, and we communicate regularly. That's the background. When my wife and two children invaded the Gonzalez home in Sacramento as houseguests a few weeks ago, we had ample time to speak about social issues. During one of our conversations, while we were isolating ourselves from four noisy children, Governor Paige of Arizona was on the phone. I heard Mike speak about a meeting to discuss people issues and asked to be included."

"Helen Reed, Reverend Domingo. Do you support the issues the governors have decided upon during the last three days?"

"Helen, you may have inside information I'm not aware of. I can and do support many of the issues discussed. I'm not aware of any decisions. These are the most patriotic and compassionate people I've ever spent time with. Because solutions to our many problems are so nebulous, I support the governors in not going public with every idea that comes up. Some are rather impractical—like insisting that automobiles be banned from city streets one day a week or having meatless days. Yet their brainstorming sessions produced some innovative thoughts."

Helen again. "Reverend Domingo, don't you think they should be more forthcoming with information? After all, they are servants of the people, spending taxpayers' money, and . . . and they are keeping us from doing our job."

"Helen, none of them would have mentioned this to you, but I will. Every single governor is personally paying his or her own expenses and those of their aides out of their own pockets. These are dedicated people deserving your praise."

"Halpert, CNN. Reverend Domingo, you could be a dominant force in any political campaign, and yet you said you could not be a politician. If you truly have so much concern for the American people, how can you avoid becoming involved?"

"I believe my work as a minister of the Gospel is involvement and the best possible service I can perform. Most of you may know of me from my television ministry. However, I still spend three-fourths of my time as a small parish pastor and my TV exposure always must come second to the needs of my own church. If you wish to know Eddy Domingo, come to our church or join one of our support groups."

Still Halpert: "Reverend Domingo, you are recognized as an evangelist who is in tune with the common people, yet you are only giving them 25 percent of your time. Wouldn't it be prudent to spend more of your time with the greater number of people?"

Domingo's smile spread all over his face. "Mr. Halpert, I accept your implied criticism. We feel the greatest need is a judgment call and only my advisers and I can make that. If you have specific information we should consider, I'd be happy to discuss it with you."

"Isn't Governor Gonzalez one of your advisers?" It was still Halpert. "Haven't you considered he might be telling you to direct your activities away from media exposure for his own political benefit?"

Domingo laughed. "Yes, Governor Gonzalez is my personal confidant and an adviser. If your scenario is correct, the people of California have been the great beneficiaries and they would join me in approbation. I think it's important that everyone understand the reason I asked to attend these meetings. I wanted to learn from experts in government what ways might be open to improve our democracy. Some of you may feel it would have been better to have an open forum with the 535 members of Congress. But they have been pushing us into a deeper mire for years. The executive branch proposes, but Congress wields the real power; you know that. If you feel I made a mistake by coming here, I'll accept that. I do hope you believe me when I say the right people are here at the right time. I will continue to listen to new thoughts from these—and other statesmen—both genders included."

"Ryan, NBC. Reverend Domingo, you have a one-hour television show tomorrow evening. Will you mention any of the ideas discussed here?"

"Since none of them has been distilled into action

points, I will defer comments on them. However, many of the thoughts raised in the brainstorming sessions are quite similar to the ideas Reverend Falwell, Reverend Robertson, Cardinal O'Connor, and I have been talking about. Please tune in."

"Marty Benton for Governors Addams and Hadley: when and where will you have your next meeting?"

Addams responded, "No time or place has been considered. We expect to contact other governors and many lawmakers before making a judgment."

"Will your next meeting be open to the press or will you hide behind some sinister cloak of secrecy?"

Hadley had a problem being civil. "Mr. Benton, there has been nothing sinister about our talks. We will not accept your rude remarks until you tell us publicly about your own personal conversations. Aih've heard you and your foul language often enough to not have much respect for y'all. For the rest of you professional reporters, aih can only tell you that if there is another group meeting to explore new ways of solving our many governmental problems, it will be up to the attendees to determine the type of forum."

Helen Reed said, "Governor, please let me apologize for some of the remarks of the media. We are frustrated because we see many governors and other political activists who have been talking about political business for nearly three days and we haven't been able to get many specifics."

"Thank you, Helen." Governor Hadley had cooled off a bit. "Possibly the mistake we made is having this press conference when we didn't have enough specific information to give you. The other governors and I have probably learned more from you this mornin' than you have from us. Thank y'all for comin'."

Marty Benton rushed up to ask Hadley and Addams a question. Flint Hadley glared at him and said in an exaggerated southern drawl, "Young fella, you are one miserable sod."

Chapter Six

The fatigued governors and their advisers adjourned to a private dining room for lunch. Some admitted the press conference might have been a mistake, but they felt nothing was said that would compromise their position or their commitment to the president.

Governor Hadley phoned President Lee. He had seen and heard the whole thing on CNN and chided his friend. "Those mousy reporters can get under your skin, can't they? Anyway, I'm anxious to sit down with you, Brad, and Mike and talk things over. When can you come up?"

"I'll phone you back just as soon as I can get to the others, Evans. Would tomorrow be OK?"

"I'll work you in whenever, so come as soon as it's convenient for all of you."

As lunch was being served, Governor Addams suggested they spend time exploring suggestions about contacting the other governors. "I also ask you, should we plan on another meeting so we might deserve more attention from the media?" There was nervous laughter.

Maine's governor, Helen Gardner, stood up to be heard. "I don't think we should be too critical of ourselves. Maybe the press conference was no piece of cake, but we did learn from it. It's not going to be practical for fifty governors to meet and not draw a lot of attention from the media. My suggestion is that each of us contact one or two governors. We should have an advisory team in the wings if needed. Not just because she's the correct gender, but because of her demonstrated ability, I hope Cynthia Spicer can be a member of that group. While I have your attention, I wish to acknowledge and thank our advisers. They did a tremendous job in making practical sense out of the many ideas that were generated." There was generous applause.

"Good suggestions, Helen." Addams went on, "Let's have names of those you'd wish on the facts squad. Also, tell us whom you will contact. After lunch, will the advisers set up some sort of reporting program and determine the best communication method for us to use? I'm pleased at the progress we've made in the past few days. I know we wish to thank Flint Hadley for his hospitality and each and every one of you for your ideas. You heard the president ask that a few of us visit him. If you wish, we'll report on that visit in a very confidential manner."

After lunch, governors and aides alike made lists of people they could contact. Three separate fact squads of three persons each were set up. Though Cynthia Spicer was included in the eastern team, she was also the general chairperson and Governor Addams agreed she work full-time on the revitalization of the Americas.

At 7:05 Thursday morning, Governors Addams, Hadley, and Gonzalez took the two-hour commercial flight to Washington. They cabbed to the White House and within minutes were in conference with President Lee. While Gonzalez had met the president on several occasions, he held the man who had the most important job in the land in genuine awe. The others were old friends. All were able to begin speaking in a sincere and friendly manner.

The president settled back in his chair and asked,

"OK, so you're the experts; how do we fix what's wrong with government?"

Flint Hadley exhaled a low growl, squirmed in his chair, and let his drawl fill the room. "Evans, aih don't believe the federal government is fixable as it's constituted. You and aih have been in politics more than forty years, and we have seen things grow progressively worse. The federal government is just too damn big. Too many people are involved, and the costs are too high! Despite your efforts and the work of many dedicated congressmen, there is really no line of communication between Washington and the people. Let me put it this way—there are three basic segments of our population.

"One: business, large and small. Businesses pay corporate taxes. Their owners/stockholders pay taxes again on the residual profits or earnings.

"Two: the massive number of wage earners who are the major supporters of our tax base.

"Three: the people who need help from a sympathetic government because they are not employed, either because they can't find work or because they are unable to work due to their particular health or social situation.

"In the past, for many more years than you and aih have been around, the federal gov-e-ment has attempted to pacify the complaints of any one of those groups by throwing money at it—to the disadvantage of the other two."

"Flint, I agree—if there were a better way, you and I would have used it. The entitlement programs choke the federal government. They grow bigger because Congress continues to demand its pork barrel benefits to get even the most necessary bills passed."

"Evans, aih told you on the phone the other evenin' that you would be a supporter of our thinkin' when you had all the facts—information, really, that you know better than most anyone else in the world."

"Mr. President," Brad Addams was speaking, "what we're talking about is something very serious. We believe that every single person at the Saddlebrook meeting is a patriot whose only wish is to solve our national predicament—the dilemma of how to represent our constituents fairly without continuing to generate a national debt so huge that it will eventually bankrupt this or any other form of government. That will not only cause a recession—it will cause a depression so severe that one can't imagine the consequences."

Mike Gonzalez, a bit nervous, managed to keep his anxiety under control. "Mr. President, could we review for you what the governors had on their minds in Florida? We'd like you to know what we will be telling governors who were not there."

The three visitors spent more than an hour briefing the president. President Lee listened intently and asked a few questions. When they finished, he exhaled completely, got out of his chair, and walked around the Oval Office. Without sitting down, he said, "You guys have one hell of a program. There are many good points in it—I wish we could adopt some of them today. All of you know what little luck I'd have trying to get any of the propositions through the Congress. I know the federal government is too big. I know it's too costly. I know we do a poor job satisfying the voters. What bothers me about your program is that it's likely to have so much appeal."

Evans Lee went to his chair and sat down heavily. "You know I must and I will fight you every step of the way. We cannot let the Union be destroyed or dissolved. We are the greatest nation in the world because we are able to speak with the authority of fifty states. We have over two hundred years of stability, except for the time when secession was on the mind of some states. Surely none of us would consider another civil war as a viable means to gain our purpose."

Mike Gonzalez, his eloquent voice moderated, said quite emphatically, "Mr. President, we certainly would not wish any civil disturbance. We believe we should take our program to the people in the form of a referendum. We understand there are many obstacles we'll likely face, but if you were to speak to each of the governors at Saddlebrook you would know how determined they are to change and how enthused they are about the proposals we've just laid out for you."

"Mike, I believe you, Brad, and Flint. It's just such a horrible thought—to break up the United States of America. For me, it's unthinkable."

"Evans," said Governor Hadley, "each of us went through the same crisis. When the purgin' stopped, we began to see things in a more practical light. We unnerstan' your position and we know you must do everything in your power to not only preserve the Union, but also maintain the status quo."

"The damned status quo—that's why you guys have me where the hair is short. I told you I must fight you, but I can't think of three men I respect more. It would be much easier for me if my opposition were people I could despise." He gave a nervous laugh. "Thanks for coming. Call me anytime to keep me informed. We will keep this discussion confidential until you have the rest of your meetings. Of course I'll go over things with the attorney general and get his advice."

As they prepared to leave, the president said, "Being in the Oval Office for more than fifteen minutes is usually questioned by the media. Just wanted to warn you—that

Benton fella from the *Times* gets under your skin, doesn't he, Flint?"

"He's managed to do that, Evans. Be talkin' to ya."

Reporters approached them as they left the White House, asking if they had statements. Governor Addams said they had a pleasant meeting with the president and had given him a report on the Saddlebrook conference. The governor added that discussions were private and on a friendly basis.

The three governors decided to rehash their program and have an early lunch. Afterward, Addams and Hadley left from Washington National while Gonzalez caught a flight out of Dulles.

Chapter Seven

Cynthia Spicer moved out of her capitol office into a nondescript building in downtown Boston. Ben helped her screen some young people to join the task force. All were enthusiastic, very bright, and disenchanted with the current status of government. She hired two men and three women. Her father personally committed himself to paying their salaries as well as the rent. She was anxious to start on what she dubbed the Socrates Society.

It was the end of February, and the weather was the pits nationwide. Squad members were asking where they should meet. Cynthia made reservations, and nine persons of the fact squad gathered at the Waldorf in New York City. Instead of a meeting room, they met in the lounge of a two-bedroom suite. Each member had an assistant, and besides Cynthia, the eastern group consisted of Berger from New York and Thomas from Florida. From the central part of the country were delegates from Illinois, Texas, and Alabama. The western group came from California, Alaska, and Arizona. All kept a low profile and worked diligently for four days. A primary need was to hammer out points that would be used in a concerted effort to give government back to the people. They developed responses to general questions such as: What happens to the FBI? Will there be a Supreme Court? Who takes over the national parks? What about the postal service? How could the eight country/states be tied together? *Will* they be tied together? What happens to the federal highway program? How do you divide the military into eight parts? Suppose a new political entity, your own country/state, decides it will not fund welfare programs? How do you protect the farmers? Do you propose eight different educational standards?

The governors began their one-on-one sessions with their neighbors, and attitudes were mixed. Some were miffed because they hadn't been invited to Saddlebrook. Others were horrified at the thought of breaking up the Union. Still, a majority were receptive to the unique ideas on how to gain more benefits from their current tax base and also to move government so much closer to the people. Quentin Jenkins of Pennsylvania and Diana Bloom of Ohio became instant zealots. Monty Edison spent half a day with Brownlee Williams and came away feeling the governor of Michigan was against him, yet before the week was out Williams phoned Edison and seemed more enthusiastic than any other politician in ages.

On the first Monday of March, the *New York Times* carried a copyrighted story about a growing movement among the states' right advocates. The story indicated that the individuals involved were mostly governors and a prominent evangelist. It went on telling they were all right-wingers and would not stop short of destroying the federal government. No names were given. The story closed with the remark: "The sinister politicians in 'State Houses' today are mostly contemptuous individuals who continuously seek ways to line their own pockets at the expense of American taxpayers."

On Wednesday, the *St. Louis Post Dispatch* carried a front-page story:

Socrates Society Promotes Secession of States

A loosely organized group of States' Righters is holding meetings in various parts of the country. Their purpose is to urge states to secede from the federal Union. Leaders of the group are Governors Edison, Addams, Hadley, and Gonzalez. They have had meetings with Pres. R. Evans Lee to explain their proposals. They admitted to the president their goal is to destroy the Union and set up autonomous states. None of the Socrates leaders was available for comment.

In a telephone conference call among the four named men, Flint Hadley said, "Well, boys, the stinky stuff hit the fan. We knew we couldn't keep it a secret very long, so aih propose it's time we really go public in a big way."

Brad Addams said, "Cynthia is the one who coined the name Socrates Society. Is that a problem?"

"Hell no," said Hadley. "Good name as any. Where do we go from here?"

"It'd be good if we could go national—like on *Meet the Press* or David Brinkley," said Edison. "Who has the best connections for such exposure? Mike, how about you? Could you get Reverend Domingo to provide a pipeline?"

"Maybe," said Gonzalez. "I'll check and be back to you before the end of the day. Would we want Eddy on the program?"

Addams answered, "I believe we'd be better served for him to come in later. This might just be the opportunity we need to break things wide open."

"Okay, governors, I'll be back to you after I contact Eddy."

On the ides of March, Govs. Flint Hadley and

Montgomery Edison were guests on *Meet the Press*. They weren't treated much like guests. Rather, the sanctimonious moderator did his best to vilify each of them in his introduction. Governor Hadley, known for his short fuse, remained calm and authoritative. He insisted none of the proponents of a change in governmental form was seditious. If they had a fault, it was in their overconcern for the American people. Governor Edison spoke in his usual suave manner, every bit the patrician who so annoyed the media. Neither skirted difficult questions and each worked in his own opinions of the great benefits of smaller government entities.

When the lady of the rapier tongue posed, "The United States is regarded as a nation of sympathy and generosity around the world. How would your fragmented state handle relief problems—say, an earthquake in Japan or a nuclear accident in France or Russia?" Flint Hadley moved forward in his chair, took a deep breath, and replied, "Do you recall the devastation in Florida and Louisiana from hurricanes? How about the Midwest floods or widespread winter storms? Even the areas of the world with only weekly newspapers heard about them. Yet how many foreign countries responded to our needs? None! You see, ma'am, we believe in the love of God's people and we will direct our fundamental efforts to those unfortunate persons at our doorstep first. Once we've solved our local problems by a much more concerned and responsible government we will once again be able to become missionaries to the world."

"Isn't that an unjust and impractical attitude to take?" asked the moderator.

Edison answered, "Governor Hadley and I arrived last evening and took a walk after dinner. Suppose you and your staff walk ten minutes from this Washington studio—in any direction. You will see the needs of our people. We spoke to your producer before this program began—he told us that none of you would dare walk in those areas without an armed guard. Any video feature stories about this very city are done under the protection of a heavy guard. What is your reaction to that, sir?"

"Governors, I am here only to ask questions."

Hadley retorted, "You seem to be hidin' behind a cloak of ignorance! Why do you feign broad knowledge on myriads of subjects and yet decline to give a simple opinion on activities only minutes from heah?"

"We have time for only one more question, Governors. How do you and your group of people plan to proceed without starting another holocaust or civil war?"

Governor Edison replied, "We will continue to refine the program, the needs of the people, and more specifically define the needs of government and then propose a referendum. In our idea of a better democracy, the people must be closer to their government so they will be the ones to decide, not we present-day politicians."

On the same Sunday, Governors Addams and Gonzalez were on ABC with David Brinkley. Brinkley introduced the pair as founding members of the Socrates Society and advisers to evangelist Eddy Domingo.

Before a question could be asked, Governor Addams said, "Sorry, David, neither statement is correct. My daughter, Cynthia Addams Spicer, and her gubernatorial advisers coined the Socrates Society name. It sounds good to me and maybe we should adopt it. Possibly you could give us some advice on that. Regarding Reverend Domingo, I would be honored to be called his adviser if only it were true. I've met him, spoken with him about social issues, and have a very high regard for the man."

Governor Gonzalez stepped in. "Eddy Domingo and I

grew up together in East Los Angeles. Our families are very close. We often exchange opinions and that could sometimes be construed as advice."

Brinkley asked, "Does Reverend Domingo support the Socrates Society plan?"

Gonzalez flashed his smile. "I don't know—I've never asked him. This could be an assignment for one of your reporters, I suppose."

"Wasn't Reverend Domingo in attendance at your meeting in Tampa?"

"Yes, he was, and he was a great contributor of ideas."

"But you don't know if he's in agreement with the Socrates program?"

Gonzalez was still answering. "If and when there is such a thing as a Socrates program, each of us will be able to decide what we can support. Our plans are dynamic, and when they have been distilled into an 'action program' all of us, including you, Mr. Brinkley, will be able to determine our support."

The lovely lady with the polished voice asked, "Will you tell us the president's reaction when you explained your ideas to him?"

Addams replied, "The president listened carefully and before we left he asked that we keep him informed of our activities. We will do that. As for his reaction—well, he is the president of the United States of America and he reminded us of that. I have a great deal of respect for President Lee. He is a close, longtime friend of Governor Hadley, and I've known and worked with him for twenty-five years. The presidency is only a part of the problem. The crux of the issue is the massive and burgeoning bureaucracy. It is not cost-effective. More often than not, the few are pork barrel politicians. Our federal government does not produce anything—well, not much anyway.

It operates the postal system and some power plants and a few other things. Yet it has more employees than the total of all our manufacturing jobs! Our central government has spread to the tiniest hamlets because bureaucratic growth appeals to so many politicians. We have 535 congressmen and -women. Each has a staff that is ridiculously large, and they do not do anything that couldn't be done better at the local level. Besides, as a group, they cost us in the neighborhood of a billion dollars a year."

Another questioner: "Aw, come on, Governor. You mean to tell us we could do away with Congress completely and the states could perform their functions?"

"Absolutely, sir. If Congress were abolished tomorrow morning, the state houses would be operating more effectively within a month. Please understand that much of the work done by state employees is to double-check on our federal friends and follow up on the often-irrational direction of congressional laws."

Brinkley asked, "What are your proposals for handling the postal service and Amtrak?"

Gonzalez said, "The government shouldn't be in those businesses now. They should be and would be privatized."

"What about the national parks? Would you suggest they be sold to private companies also?"

"No, ma'am, the various country/states should take them over and operate them more efficiently and less costly. We feel people will have a greater feeling of personal possessiveness when things are run as they should be. Our parks, like our cities, will have an opportunity for rebirth because there will be more funds available without ramming through tax increases."

"Governor Gonzalez, do you favor any sort of tax increase? How else can the budget deficit be resolved?"

"Sir, I do favor a tax increase on motor fuel. Most of

our oil is imported, and our gasoline prices are less than half those in any other industrialized country. I cannot tell you what our advisory council will advocate concerning the present gargantuan national debt, but I prefer it be divided up on a population basis. The new country/states will be in a better position to retire their share of the debt than the present federal government with its constant logjam of conflicting issues."

Brinkley asked, "Governors, you seem to have ready answers for each of the issues; are you prepared to go to the country now?"

Governor Addams responded, "David, we have answers for those questions you and your staff asked. I fear we are still short of solutions on many points. We are seeking help from some of the top military minds for practical advice regarding not only the armed forces, but also the whole military complex."

"Isn't it true that both of you are pacifists and that Governors Hadley and Edison are as well?"

Addams smiled faintly. "Sir, I've never thought of us as pacifists. Surely our records tell you we aren't when it comes to defense from an outside force. If preferring peace to war labels me a pacifist, then please put the sticker on me. I do not believe the United States or the state of Massachusetts or the new country/state my constituents fall in should be a policeman to the world."

The pretty lady asked, "Governor Addams, we know you intend to divide the nation into eight small countries. I live in Stamford; do you know where I'll be living?"

Addams snickered. "Not unless you wish to tell me?"

"I mean, governor, which of your new country/states will my state be relegated to?"

"From memory, I believe Connecticut would be included in the proposed Confederation of New England.

The task force will be working on that very issue next week."

Brinkley did the wrap-up: "Governor Addams, Governor Gonzalez, thank you for coming. I feel we will be hearing much about you and from you in the coming months."

*　*　*

Eddy Domingo's Easter Sunday "Sunrise Service" was carried for one hour by the three major networks as well as CNN. Estimates were that more than 40 million persons watched this spectacle. The choir was made up of a battery of singing stars, and their renditions of the hymns were breathtaking. When Reverend Domingo moved out to center stage, the huge auditorium crowd fell into a hushed silence.

"I wish to speak to you about our Risen Savior—about a Man who actually rose from the dead. I want to talk about our love of God and how that enriches our life. But most of all on this special day for all Christians, I wish to help us understand how much God loves us." Then, for thirty-three minutes, Eddy Domingo responded to his calling. The congregation laughed and they shed tears. They nodded their heads in affirmation at things their minister said. As he was finishing, Domingo grew more serious, even somber. "We Christians look to Christ for guidance. We petition Him and we know He will respond to us. Those of you who are not Christians still look to your God for blessings and know that His love flows in abundance. All of us—no matter which religion we've been given or have chosen on our own—must know that the most important way to satisfy God's will is to prove our love for Him. How do we do that? By loving one another!

72

I hope you'll be with us next week when I will explain a new and exciting way for us to better love and serve our neighbors. May God bless each of you."

Gov. Miguel Gonzalez and his family visited the Domingo family in Newport Beach for the Easter holidays. The governor left that information on his answering machine. The mistake cost him Easter Sunday peace. Calls came from nearly every state. Politicians and media people alike had similar questions: "Is Evangelist Eddy Domingo going to support us publicly?" or from the media: "Is Domingo coming out for secession?" Since Eddy had not discussed the matter with Mike, it was easy for the governor to tell each caller, "Reverend Domingo and I do not discuss the topics for his sermons. I will watch him on the tube next Sunday." That reply satisfied no one, but Gonzalez persisted even to Flint Hadley and Brad Addams.

*   *   *

The Sunday after Easter, Evangelist Domingo's TV sanctuary was draped with flags. One American flag stood to the right of the pulpit. The others were of various states in the Union.

As the sound of the choral group diminished into a soft whisper, the congregation broke into applause and Eddy Domingo walked briskly to the lectern. The TV monitors strategically located throughout the church registered the engaging smile while he stood motionless waiting for his flock to settle down.

"God is always with us. This morning, I feel His hand on my shoulder. Sit back and relax so you will be able to sense Christ touching you."

There was mass movement in the pews and then shouts of, "Amen!" It was incredible, but many were saying

73

"I can really feel Him touching me." Others gasped and said, "It is the hand of God; it really is!"

Domingo did not read from the Scriptures as he normally opened his sermon. "Now that we have proof that Jesus, our God, is right here with us in our tabernacle, we know how important it is to open our minds and learn how to better love and serve Him. We must put into practice Christ's own teachings, love one another. We know it's easier for us to say 'love' than it is to make it part of our routine, part of daily life. When each of us came into our humble building this morning, we couldn't help noticing the street people near the entrances. Did we ignore them or did we show compassion? No one ever said it would be easy to follow in Christ's footsteps." For twenty-eight minutes Eddy Domingo spoke of the many things people must do to prove their love of God and the great reward they would receive for being a soldier, a follower of Jesus.

"I would like to take the rest of our time to discuss with you something that is very serious. It's the way we are governed. I may need to pinch time from our wonderful choir in order to convey my thoughts. A few months ago some dedicated and patriotic people spoke to me about a proposal for a massive change in the way we rule ourselves in this democratic society. Those men implied that we, you and I, would be better served by eliminating the federal government—that's correct; they suggested breaking up the Union. They felt we citizens would be better off without the bureaucratic confusion of Washington. They told me that localized government could do everything better and less expensively than the politicians who inhabit the halls of Congress. 'Break up the Union?' I asked. 'You mean you wish to throw away more than two hundred years of glorious history?' The idea horrified me! They gave me their thoughts and asked me to reflect on them.

"Last month I attended a meeting in Florida with more than twenty governors who wished to discuss ways to improve our government. There were many constructive ideas, and the central theme was how to bring government closer to the American people. The thoughts generated there are being distilled by a group of brilliant young professional people who will very shortly present to all of us their ideas on how to carry out a revolutionary way to vastly improve our democracy. I want you to know that I support the proposals I've heard so far. I believe our government has moved too far away from us. It is time for you and me to tell the federalists we wish to regain government of the people . . by the people . . . and for the people."

"Localized government means government by men and women in your own communities—close to the people they govern. Each area would determine its taxation requirements based on local needs. An agricultural area might feel the need to support farmers while a wholly industrial location would cater to the specific needs of its own people.

"The centralized or federal government has generated a massive bureaucracy that has grown faster than the largest employers in the country. You know how cumbersome it is, how slow it is to react, and how inept it is at solving our problems."

Domingo spent the rest of his evangelical hour telling how much better government would be when American lives were not dictated from Washington.

"Congress, the legislative branch, makes laws for the 'average' man, woman, and child. You and I know there are no 'average persons.' The honorable men and women in Congress and their thousands of assistants try to be fair to everyone in all fifty states. What is fair to those of you in New Orleans or Dallas or Phoenix may not be at all fair to those of you who live in New York or Boston. What is equitable for farmers in Kansas may not be right for the vegetable growers in California. Oftentimes those discrepancies are resolved by special subsidies, sometimes referred to as pork barrel projects.

"Most of your taxes are 'federal taxes.' The central government collects tax money so that it can operate. It must also send funds back to the states so local governments can provide needed services. Rarely is enough money returned to states and municipalities for them to operate without assessing a tax burden of their own.

"What should we do? We aren't certain yet. If you were to speak to your local governor or mayor, he or she would likely tell you that a good portion of their governmental expense is in verifying and carrying out directives imposed by Washington. So, I ask you, do we need the federal bureaucracy? Do we need an enormous and expensive staff of people in Washington on our payroll to direct our lives? I'm not at all certain—I don't believe so!

"What is the alternative? It could be the complete elimination of the federal government! How would that work? State and local governments would take over the services now performed under Washington's directives. That's cutting out the middleman. You know that would save a whole lot of our money!"

In the last two minutes, he asked his parishioners and the television audience to prayerfully study the issues. He closed by saying, "When we learn how much we will all equally benefit from a closer-knit, more localized government, we should demand a referendum so every one of us—the voters representing all 260 million people—can speak with a clarion voice. May God bless us all."

Supporters of Domingo's ideas and others believing in

what they'd heard about the Socrates Society were pleased. Most people were irritated because an evangelist was getting involved in politics. Nearly every congressional member was critical of the whole idea of secession. The media was pleased! It had a new issue to fill its time slots and ink its pages.

Not all governors declared their preference publicly; a few retained a strong opinion that the federal government should survive in its present form.

Both the Democratic and Republican parties began active campaigns for the preservation of the Union. Each planned gigantic programs for the Fourth of July. The Democrats chose "Patriotism and the Union" as their theme. The Republicans chose "One Nation—Indivisible." In thirty-one state capitals, the Socrates followers had minidemonstrations with each governor explaining the advantage of home rule and deploring taxation with inadequate representation. The country was becoming more divided, and anxiety in the White House was as great as in Congress.

On July 7, the leaders of the United States, England, France, Germany, Russia, Italy, Japan, and Korea met in Berlin to discuss mutual economic and political problems. President Lee was asked repeatedly about the divisive tactics in his country, and he admitted concern. On the second day of the summit meeting, one of President Lee's sons was tragically killed in an auto accident. The president flew home immediately.

The Berlin Summit felt it could do little without the American president. However, they did produce a declaration supporting the status of a federal government in the United States and criticized the radical element that proposed a breakup of the Union.

In a news conference, the prime ministers of England,

Germany, and Japan had harsh remarks for the American politicians who would disrupt the balance of a world economy. Even worse, without the cloak of a U.S. military power in readiness, their own countries could be in jeopardy.

Every major newspaper in the U.S. headlined "Foreign Interference" in some fashion. The liberal news commentators pounded the three countries for daring to become involved in U.S. affairs.

The governors committed to change took advantage of the rhetoric on both sides and became more definitive on their ideas for local government. Men like Hadley, Addams, Edison, Gonzalez, Brown, and Davis took the wraps off their programs and for the first time advocated secession. By the first of August, the national polls began to show a high percentage of voters favoring the elimination of the federal government.

Cynthia Addams Spicer reported to her father that their platform was complete enough for presentation to the fifty governors. She recommended copies be sent to each, as well as to President Lee. As a final point, she told Brad, "Dad, we feel it's time for the lawyers to present the document to a United States District Court, asking that it be placed on the November ballot."

*   *   *

Peter Brandt, graying at the temples and deeply tanned from working in the vineyard, was clearly the leader. At forty-five, he was also the oldest of the five men around the kitchen table in a middle-class home near Fresno City College. Mark Gest, a few years younger and a German-language instructor, was short and thin and wore thick-lensed specs. He had little hair to color. The other three were in their early twenties—and they were skinheads. Each was blond, athletic, aggressive, and with total disregard for anyone else. They were Bobby Gardner, Max Owens, and Billy Simpson.

Peter Brandt was saying, "Now is a good time to make an explosive impact on the fools trying to take over this country. We could wipe out the big spick in Sacramento. He has no respect for any white people, much less true Aryans."

"Pete," Mark Gest said, "silencing Gonzalez is a good idea—but you know what? Eddy Domingo would be a better target. He is the *numero-uno* spick. He's on TV regularly, and his theme is always the equality of mankind. I'd personally like to strangle the toothy bastard."

Bobby Gardner snarled when he talked; he felt it gave him status. "Damned right. Me 'n' Max 'n' Billy could get that Jesus man anytime. Want us to go to his church in LA and feed him some lead?"

Brandt smiled. "Yeah, Domingo is a better target. Anyways, it's no good for you guys to do the job. Geez, the whole country would be on our ass. How 'bout contracting the work out?"

"Sure. OK, Pete," said Bobby. "Me 'n' the guys could go to LA 'n' hire some gooks to take care of him."

Gest stared through his thick lenses. "It would be better to make the attack away from California. I agree on having others do him in so our own goals are not compromised and we'd still reap the benefits. We must let the world know that we are superior! Those browns and blacks and yellows are not equal."

"Who would do it?" asked Max Owens.

"Many people—for money. Mafia guys, Arabs, Jews, maybe some Asians. Hey, even some cops wanta make extra money. What do you think, Mark?" asked Pete.

"I'm sure you're right, Pete," Mark said. "You three young men could check things out in Chicago, Detroit, New York, or Miami. Those places have all the ethnic groups, and none of them are happy."

Brandt was elated. He could see an action plan hatching. "OK, guys, do that. See what sort of a deal can be made. Don't mention who the target guy is. Find a trigger man and see how much it will cost. Sure be good to rid the world of Domingo or even Gonzalez, 'n' I like the idea of somebody doin' the job for us."

Chapter Eight

The U.S. District Court in Cincinnati refused to hear the referendum issue. Cynthia Spicer was pleased—now it could go to the U.S. Supreme Court, where it belonged.

Every politician and legal expert knew it would be impossible to get the Supreme Court to authorize a referendum for the November ballot. Many felt the Court might even refuse to consider an issue that amounted to the elimination of the United States of America as a nation.

The petition was placed on the court agenda during the first week of the fall session. The chief justice passed around copies of the brief prepared by the Socrates Society lawyers saying, "You are free to read this at your leisure. I suppose the best time might be when you are hopelessly constipated."

At the December recess, not a single word was mentioned among the justices regarding the referendum permitting states to secede from the federal Union. One thought was that it had been buried for good.

Congress adjourned for the holiday season, and most members felt the secession issue had been put to rest for a good long time.

The Reverend Eddy Domingo had just finished putting the wraps on his Christmas spectacular. Gov. Miguel Gonzalez was to be one of his guests; others included actors, musicians, singers—all dedicated to the right of the states to be free. On the stage was a reasonable replica of the Statue of Liberty. The Lady was in shackles, her usual pleasant face in a grimace. Her torch would flicker, then go out, and when that happened the electronic sign with her full name, "Liberty Enlightening the World," would also blink out.

Domingo's homily was on the good news of the coming of the Savior, the God child, sent to redeem the world. This was a baby born of a virgin mother through the power of God. Then Eddy spoke of God's great love for his people. "God loves us the same today as He did thousands of years ago, and He asks so very little from us to keep His graces showering down upon us. He has particularly blessed this land, and we know He wishes us to take the greatest possible advantage of the resources he has placed at our disposal.

"Surely Jesus has a twinge of disappointment at the way bureaucrats in our government are so wasteful. It is for that reason that I ask you to speak in a loud and forceful voice to demand the opportunity for every one of our states to move out from under a repressive and archaic federalism into a new confederation that does, in fact, provide for a true form of democratic government. We must have a governmental environment we can afford that still enables us to serve the needs of our people.

"The Supreme Court must authorize a referendum soon so we can answer God's call."

Other evangelists played on the secession theme. The man in central Virginia spoke of how the fumbling bureaucrats in Washington had infiltrated the lives of Americans, making them slaves to the federal government. He said, "We have gone from a shaky and weak central government before the time of George Washington to the present invasive federalism. Another Abraham Lincoln would surely have the answer—he would sign an Emancipation

Proclamation freeing *us,* the serfs." In word and song, his program praised the Socrates Society document and urged the Court to permit a referendum on the issue of establishing a confederation of American states on the very next national ballot.

A gigantic Christmas show from the Hollywood Bowl was really a fund-raiser for the Socrates issue. Guests included former president Clayton Farrington, former senator Herbert Fullman, Governor Gonzalez, and Rev. Eddy Domingo. All received heartening applause. The entertainers had been selected for their diversity in race and creed. Eighteen members of Congress were part of the enthusiastic audience.

After the holidays, the media began fill-in programs on the Socrates agenda. While many denounced the very thought of a breakup of the federal government, still there were many supporters. To be sure, the idea was radical, and yet many members of Congress were obviously in favor of sweeping changes.

More than two-thirds of the nation's governors supported all or at least a part of the Socrates program. Federal and state politicians and employees began polarizing their points of view.

Pres. R. Evans Lee savagely attacked the idea of secession in his State of the Union address. "People who favor the ideas of the Socrates Society are interested in their own personal gain, not the welfare of our 260 million people. They wish to destroy more than two hundred years of model government and take this country back to the dark ages of some unworkable feudal system. If they have their way, the standard of living of our people will only be that of a Third World country. We cannot, we will not, let them do that to us."

Each weekend was marked by demonstrations. Both

sides had prominent advocates, and the entertainment spectacles helped weld the groups together.

The U.S. Supreme Court agreed to hear the States' Rights Amendment in early February. The U.S. government lawyers were accompanied by an unusually large number of advisers. The Socrates or Confederation group was equally well represented. Testimony ran into the second day. Then, the tension mounted while the entire country began the agonizing wait for the Court's ruling.

*　　*　　*

Proponents of each side were respectfully quiet during the expected two-week period awaiting a decision. Not the public in general, however. There were town meetings and demonstrations day after day. The issues didn't change:

- Preservation of the Union
- States' rights
- "We are the United States of America"
- Government of the people, by the people, for the people
- Avoidance of civil war
- Peace and justice through confederation
- Home rule
- Patriots for confederation
- Federalism is bondage

The media reported stories of the major demonstrations rather accurately, yet many readers of the news yielded to pressure groups or their own egos and began slanting stories. The public became infuriated, and adherents on each side threatened to boycott advertisers if the "know-it-all" newscasters didn't report accurately. All four networks put major news anchors on vacation rather than jeopardize their revenue base.

On March 3, the U.S. Supreme Court failed to announce a ruling. Wild stories sprang up throughout the country:

- The court refused to rule on the issue.
- The court cannot reach a majority ruling because of abstentions.
- The chief justice recommended to the associate justices that they defer until the president has an opportunity to appoint a new justice who could change the balance in favor of federalism.

*   *   *

On April 12, the U.S. Supreme Court surprised millions of people, especially most of the federally elected politicians. In a 4–3 decision, with two abstentions, the court ruled that each state had the right to secede from the federal Union to form a confederation providing the issue be approved by a majority of the state's voters. A referendum was authorized and approved for the first Tuesday after the first Monday in the following November.

The majority opinion was written by Chief Justice Hugo Warren: "Our founding fathers protested against intolerable acts. It would be wrong to deny such determination in the twenty-first century. Chief Justice John Marshall pointed out early in the nineteenth century that the Constitution was 'intended to endure for ages to come, and, consequently, to be adapted to the various crises of human affairs.' It is, therefore, proper that the governed be given the opportunity to have their voices heard."

There were cries of jubilation and of agony. Newspaper headlines registered their strong opinions: "CHANCE TO BE FREE" ; "FREE AT LAST"; "HOME RULE POSSIBLE"; "IMPEACH THE COURT"; "CIVIL WAR LOOMS".

Fifty states were each to have their own voice on continued federalism or secession to form a coalition or confederation. No matter what the outcome of the November vote was, it was obvious that Washington, D.C., would no longer maintain a stranglehold on the lives of 260 million Americans.

President Lee called an emergency cabinet meeting to confer on the grave constitutional issue. The secretary of state and the chairman of the Joint Chiefs of Staff took a very belligerent attitude. The five-star general said, "By God, we won't let 'em break up the Union. I don't give a damn how many votes those fascists get."

Secretary of State Forest Mathers agreed. "We can get an injunction to keep the issue off the ballot. If we're beaten there, we'll swarm the courts with enough crap to keep the Socrates traitors in limbo for a hundred years."

The president looked at each and then in a weary but positive voice said, "Is that your idea of how our democracy should work? I think not! Maybe it's such opinions that put us in our present position. We serve at the will of the people—maybe we've forgotten that!"

Lee turned to his assistant, Sherman Roberts, "Sherm, work with these people to put together our side of the story. We owe it to the people and to the heritage of this country to present our views on the advantages of federalism and how much the citizens will lose if the Union is destroyed. Better get the best media help available and pull in all the help you need. Don't sell the Socrates Society short. I know many of the leaders personally, and they are not traitors—they are patriots determined to break up the massive bureaucracy we have grown here in Washington and . . . and throughout the country."

"Mr. President," asked Roberts, "you know Hadley and Addams very well. How do you read the situation? Any advice on what sort of tactics we should employ?"

"I would feel much better if Cynthia Spicer were sitting in here with us. She will put together a very appealing program, an honest assessment of the issues and a fervent appeal that will be hard to criticize. I believe it would be unwise to attack the integrity of any of the Socrates leaders. Even Clay Farrington is on their side; imagine a former president and leader of our own party. Better to go for the united theme: two hundred years of stability, world power, leader of the free world, that sort of thing. A breakup would mean that many of the new confederation units would surely be insignificant in the new world order. Does that help?"

"Yes," Roberts said. He turned to the others in the room and said, "Let's get to work. We have one hell of a job in front of us."

The nation's governors met in New York City in mid-May for a three-day session. They asked their advisory group to attend—it had grown from the original nine to fifty-two, so that every state was represented as well as Puerto Rico and Guam.

Gov. Flint Hadley chaired the conference with the announced purpose of hearing the voices of all states. It was a somber group of male and female chief executives who had fateful decisions to make. The sixteen governors who violently objected to secession and confederation still agreed in principle to an overwhelming number of issues raised by the Socrates group. Their points of view were given weighty consideration.

At the end of the first day, a special gubernatorial judicial committee passed on to the advisory group a list of items that required urgent attention. They included:

- Reduction of costs of government
- Ways to be more attentive to issues and provide better services
- Quick elimination of the burden of the national debt
- Privatization of as much of the government as possible
- Options for the makeup of the confederation
- A detail procedure to invite certain non–U.S. states or provinces to join Confederation
- Development of educational programs that provide for retraining of federal workers and discharged military personnel
- Outline of options for the best use of the military

Cynthia Addams Spicer was appointed chairperson of the Socrates Society, and during the following two days the advisers were divided into committees to study and report back on specific issues. Headquarters would be moved to Kansas City. They had less than a month to provide a constructive program for the governors' meeting in mid-June. A new element was being added. Seven U.S. senators were given permission for aides to be included as well as staff personnel of eighteen House members.

Much discussion, among both the governors and their advisers, centered on how to treat states that did not vote authorization to secede. Could they join the confederation at a later date? If they remained a part of the old Union, how would they be governed, taxed, financed, or represented to foreign governments? What should their relationship be toward the confederation?

Cynthia discussed the matter with her father, and he

vowed to speak to the president to get his thoughts concerning that particular detail when he and Governor Hadley phoned him at the end of the conference.

Cynthia's thoughts were that they would indeed remain a part of the Union. They would support the Union financially and decide among themselves on a relationship with the new federation. Eighteen of the governors favored continuation of the Union or federal membership. Their battery of advisers was immediately given the task of developing their own strategic programs.

As the conference was ending, Flint Hadley reminded all the governors of his promise to phone the president and report on the happenings. The Florida chief executive suggested it could be a conference call so anyone could have his or her voice heard. On Wednesday afternoon at 4:00 EDT, the call was made to Pres. R. Evans Lee.

"Mr. President," drawled Hadley, "we're windin' up the governors' conference and aih'm calling to give you a report on what's transpired. First off, let me tell you what the numbers look like. You know we are represented by Puerto Rico and Guam as well as all fifty states in the federation. Five governors could not attend, but they sent representatives. In four cases, it's the lieutenant governor. Evans, it appears to me that eighteen favor the Union and thirty-four favor confederation. As aih told your secretary, those who wished to be a part of this call are plugged in so they can speak to you directly. Before aih let them do that, aih do want you to know again that what's happenin' is somethin' aih could never have dreamed of in a thousand years. Yet . . . Mr. President, aih believe that if you were to hear everything these men and women have had to say, well, Evans Lee would also favor confederation."

"Flint, thank you for the courtesy of your call and the opportunity for me to speak to our fine governors. Each of you knows that our pledge of allegiance is to the United States of America, one nation, indivisible—it hurts me immensely that even one of you considers the option of secession.

"It's difficult for me to believe that you have studied the full ramifications there would be in breaking our country into fifty separate countries. Our status as a world power would evaporate, and just as surely as we are speaking here, the standard of living of our citizenry would tumble drastically. You can't have solved all the issues of any sort of independence in so short a time. I ask you to postpone this proposed referendum until we have had time to delve into every nook and cranny of government. I know our federal government can be fixed. If you feel I'm the problem, tell me and I'll resign. I will do anything within my power to preserve the Union."

"Mr. President, this is Diana Bloom of Ohio. I did not attend the previous meeting of the governors. When the various topics were discussed with me by Governor Edison, I hung up on him. I told Monty at the time that the very idea was seditious and I would not listen to any such radical ideas. I came to New York to defend my country and to denounce anyone who believed in secession or confederation. No one twisted my arm and not a single person asked me to change my mind. I had myriads of questions, and every one of them has been answered politely, intelligently, and with the concern of true patriots. I love our country . . . I love our people, and . . . and, Mr. President, I am now convinced that our people will be better governed by the confederation."

Lee asked, "Is Eddy Domingo there?"

Brad Addams said, "Mr. President, the Reverend Domingo couldn't attend. I'm not aware if anyone has spoken to him."

"Mike Gonzalez, have you been in touch with Eddy?"

"No, Mr. President. Eddy is on an evangelistic tour of Europe. He was to be at Wembley Stadium in London this week—last night, I believe. Then he has engagements in Norway and Sweden."

"It's rather urgent that I speak to him, Mike. Could you have him phone me?"

"Certainly, Mr. President."

"Mr. President, this is Quent Jenkins." The popular governor of Pennsylvania had been a reluctant supporter of confederation. "I told you only a few weeks ago that I would never go along with that Socrates bunch of crackpots. Well, sir, I'm here to tell you they are the most intelligent people I've had the pleasure of being with in a very long time. You are not the problem, Mr. President, but the federal system is. It's the bureaucracy; it's the remoteness of government. It's the political system of the whole damn world that has latched onto us. We can no longer afford to be a rich uncle while we have millions of people in Pennsylvania and every other state that need help. Congress is not going to fix the problems. Even if they could, they wouldn't want to. You know that Ronald Reagan said government couldn't solve the problem because government *is* the problem. Every single person I've spoken to loves his or her country very deeply. They love our people much more and, Evans Lee, they are dedicated to a renewed form of government that will make us all very proud in the future. I am with them 100 percent and I am willing to lay my life on the line for this cause."

"Thanks for your point of view, Quint. Flint said there were eighteen of you against secession. What have you to say in my defense?"

"Rod Farris, Mr. President. I cannot visualize the state of Virginia not being in the United States of America.

91

I believe in statehood for Puerto Rico—even Guam if they wish it. But you know what, Mr. President? When this comes to a vote, you and I will go down to defeat in Virginia. What is being proposed has too much merit to be denied. However, sir, I'll work my heart out with you and for the preservation of the Union, even knowing it's not the best thing for our people, because I am a federalist who believes our greatness is because all states speak as one."

"Thanks, ladies and gentlemen; you make it sound as if I'm up the creek without a paddle. I *will not* give up!"

"Flint, I hope you'll get Brad, Mike, and Eddy together and come see me very soon. Thanks to every one of you for your candor."

Foreign governments were dismayed at what was happening in America. Never before had a democratic form of government been dismantled through the free election process. Many expressed downright fear—especially those countries that had benefited from outright financial support. Others were concerned about losing the military umbrella in Europe and in the Pacific. There was also the concern that the largest open market in the world might close or at least be placed under a veil of tariff barriers or protectionist import duties.

The governors of Hawaii, California, Texas, Florida, and New York met in Kansas City with the confederation advisory group. Under the guidance of Cynthia Spicer and in the name of the Socrates Society, they issued a press release:

There are nearly 30 million Americans living below the poverty line in our fifty states. We are committed to raising their living standards to an acceptable level.

Once the new confederation of states has achieved a

prosperous, healthy populace and robust economy, it will become an ideal world partner.

Our generous Americans will continue to share with their less fortunate brothers at home and abroad, though our first priority will be at home.

Governor Gonzalez raised the question: "Shouldn't we say more? That hardly answers the fears of Japan, Russia, Israel, or Germany. Wouldn't it be appropriate to say we'll resume foreign aid when our social and economic problems are solved?"

"Aih suppose we could," said Governor Hadley. "But why? Let's not promise a thing. Our problems are more social than economic; you tell me when we've had outside help from those othah countries. Sure, France more than two hundred years ago. Mike, it might be a good ideah if some of those countries worry a bit—or a lot. Uncle Sugah should wish to clean up things at home, and that will take quite a few yearhs. Agree?"

Flint Hadley and Mike Gonzalez flew to Washington from Kansas City for a rendezvous with Brad Addams before meeting with the president. The patrician from Massachusetts was so very proud of his daughter and pleased at the praise his friends gave her. However, he was not prepared for the president's remarks.

"Brad, I wish we had Cynthia on our side. That girl has more brains in her little fingers than all my staff together. She must have had a brilliant mother."

"She did, Mr. President; thankfully, Cynthia is like her mom, or she'd be a plodder like me."

"I don't agree with that. I'd put you in second place, and as a matter of fact, I'd give you your choice of any damn cabinet post right now. I suppose—uh—Cynthia Spicer,

Eddy Domingo, and the three of you might have the talent to bring down the Union. Why can't you see it's wrong?"

"It isn't, Evans," said Flint Hadley. "What we've been sayin' about the Union is correct. Our brand of federalism is archaic because we've built up a bureaucracy that is feedin' on itself. Each new Congress comes in with a pledge to reduce government and be better representatives to the people. By the time the new members find housing outside the District, and are settled in their offices, they have joined the senior parasites in running for reelection. Of course they come in with good intentions! Certainly they intend to be good representatives of the people, but after their first day on the job they realize any correction of the problems is an impossibility. Please don't think our attitude is just a knee-jerk opinion. We aren't hip-shootin' politicians. We agonized over the situation days upon days. Our only goal was to find a solution to the problems facing fifty states. Aih wish aih could walk out of this impressive office and be able to tell the reporters at the gate that we have been foolin' the president about a referendum and that the idea of a confederation of states forming a new order was just a joke. Evans, you are the best friend aih've ever had in mah life and aih do not want to hurt you—what can aih do? Ya want me to take the gas pipe?"

"Whatever happens, Flint, we'll still be friends. Anyway, you know I have to do everything in my power to save the Union. If the election were held next week, what's your projection of the outcome?"

Addams replied, "Mr. President, I now feel that thirty-eight states would vote for the confederation. Since the election is more than four months off, that number could change to forty-two or even forty-four or even down to thirty. Many of those against us in principle—be it tradition or fear of change—are gradually understanding the seriousness of our present governmental problems."

"Mr. President, did Eddy Domingo phone you as you asked?"

"He did, Mike, thanks to you. I asked Eddy, in the name of patriotism, if he could refrain from promoting the Socrates program—even if he didn't support the union. I told him I'd be ever so pleased if he could remain neutral. Eddy only hesitated a moment before telling me I was asking something he could not do. He said he feels it's his duty to express his honest opinion. He has some sort of revival at Madison Square Garden on July Fourth and I was hoping he would stick to religion, but I guess he's going to zap us really hard. Do you know anything about his program?"

"No, Mr. President. We've never discussed his sermons. Even when I appeared on his shows I was never privy to his messages."

R. Evans Lee showed great signs of weariness. His eyes were red from lack of sleep. He was pale, evidencing his lack of time under the sunlamp. His movements were slow—almost mechanical. Hadley, his lifetime friend, said, "Evans, why don't y'all get out of this tomb for a week or two and recharge your batteries? You and aih both must let this issuh take its course. Aih don't think there is anything either of us can do at this time to change the outcome of the voting. Most people have made up their minds—one way or another. Whatever happens, y'all must remain a vibrant and effective voice in the world."

"Friend Flint, I wish I could take your good advice. My cabinet officers and the populace who believe as I do would take that as a sign of running away from the fight. I must stay here and battle for the Union—I desperately want to beat the hell out of you pragmatists."

$$* \quad * \quad *$$

In Fresno, Billy Simpson and his friends were elated over the results of their trip. In visiting friends of the shaved-head community in Chicago and Detroit, they were able to arrange contacts in New York City.

When they reported to Brandt and Gest on their trip, Snarlin' Bob Gardner was not too pleased. "We met this chick in Brooklyn: Elena Covado. First thing, Billy has her in the sack."

Simpson interrupted, "She wouldn't even listen to us 'til after I gave her a bit of lovin'. What the hell, I only did it for the cause."

"Finish your story, Bob," said Pete Brandt.

"Anyways, Elena got the hots for Billy. We'd met her brother, Raul Sanchez, in Chicago and now she's on the phone to him for advice. He says it's OK for us to meet her boyfriend. This guy, Sadam Hilali, wit' lots of hair 'n' a beard, gets real excited. If we supply the money, he will furnish the guy to take care of Domingo. Sadam says he has a cop in his pocket who will do anything for cash. We asked the cop's name and wanted to meet him. Hilali says, no way; that's his private source of income. He wouldn't give us anything on the cop."

Max Owens said, "Hilali seems on the level to me. The cop wants half a million for the hit, and Sadam and his friends want another half a million. Can we get that kinda cash, Pete?"

Brandt replied, "That's a lot of money. Mark and I should meet those people. If they can perform, we might raise the dough. What do you think, Mark?"

Gest hesitated, then replied, "I have this friend at the Pentagon. Hans Mueller is a computer genius. I don't know how he does it, but he can raise cash very quickly."

Peter Brandt and Mark Gest flew to Washington the next morning. They met Mark's friend for dinner and in a very direct conversation told Mueller their story.

"Sounds like a good idea to me," Mueller said. "That kook, Domingo, is trying to destroy the federal government. I can get you some money, but . . . a million . . . no way. Those jerks don't know how much money that is anyway. How much do you have access to now?"

"Two hundred grand," said Gest.

"OK, I'll have another 200 for you in two, maybe three days. Call me soon as you meet the people in New York."

Brandt and Gest took the train to Penn Station the following morning, and by noontime they were meeting with Elena Covado. She arranged for the three of them to have dinner with Sadam Hilali in a Queens restaurant near LaGuardia Airport and close to his apartment.

The Californians were impressed with Halali. He was literate, he claimed to have connections, and he was extremely personable. "I'll give my guarantee in blood. We will eliminate Domingo for you on July Fourth while he's in Madison Square Garden. The price is $1 million—in cash."

"Everything sounded good up to this point," said Brandt. "We have less than half that amount to spend."

Hilali laughed. "OK, so we're negotiating. Tell ya what. I can get the job done for a half a million."

"Look," Mark said. "We have 200 now. That's all. We have a promise of one or two more. That's it. Deal?"

Hilali stared at them a long time. "You aren't as serious as I thought. Anyway, I like you; let me make a phone call."

While Hilali was on the phone, Elena told them, "Sadam is a very serious man. He is accumulating funds to help the poor people in his country."

"What is his real business?" asked Brandt.

"He is an importer of olive oil, dates, and other food items from the Middle East. Sometimes he brings in Persian carpets through Lebanon."

Hilali was all smiles when he returned to the table. "I have a job guarantee for 300 grand. Course there's nothing in it for us—except satisfaction. I'll pay 150 down and the balance on July 5. Get me the cash tomorrow. OK?"

They shook hands—a done deal. Elena left with Brandt and Gest. She spent the night with Pete.

Before delivering cash to Hilali, Brandt, and Gest had time to celebrate. They had secured a contract for a reasonable amount of money, and there would be no way to trace the activities to the neo-Nazis of California.

Chapter Nine

The government media blitz started on July 1. Newspaper, magazine, and television commercials carried the same theme: "*Anarchy* is political disorder and violence: it is lawlessness."

Usually included with the copy were scenes of hand-to-hand combat, often interspersed with racial slurs. Nearly all were included—Jews, Catholics, blacks, Hispanics, and Asians.

The ads were ripe for an answer, and on July Fourth the Reverend Eddy Domingo and his Evangelistic Hour moved into Madison Square Garden. The network broadcast was scheduled for ninety minutes. The Garden was packed two hours before air time. Choral groups entertained the congregation, and dozens of visiting celebrities were introduced.

At 8:00 P.M. EST the televised show began. The athletes who made the Garden their workplace introduced singer after singer. In a departure from ordinary religious programming, some of the most hilarious comics provided laughs while ridiculing the federalist advertisements. Dancers graced the stage in a symphony of sound and motion. The house enjoyed the show.

At exactly 8:31 a hush settled over the audience. All lights dimmed and then the spotlighted figure of Eddy Domingo moved to center stage. He raised his arms in greeting and then broke into a glorious smile. People rose to their feet and shouted repeatedly, "Ed-dy! Ed-dy! Ed-dy!"

Domingo spoke of patriotism and how close it is to the love of God. Sin is bad—love is good. His voice varied in tone and in volume. At times, people in the Garden had difficulty hearing his whispers and were ever so pleased when he rose to a shout. At the end of thirty minutes, lights picked out the glistening perspiration on his beaming face. His voice was a bit weaker, but more mellow. People were mesmerized by the words he spoke.

"Before I give you back to some of our wonderful entertainers this evening, I'd like to remind you that it is your duty to learn all the facts concerning the referendum coming up this November. You are being asked to decide if you wish the United States federal Union to continue as it is—or to change to a form of government that more adequately represents you, its people. We, who favor a confederation of states without the burden of Washington, are not anarchists, as the bureaucracy is trying to paint us. Rather, we are the patriots who are fighting for a government of the people, by you, the people, and for you, the people. As a single individual, I tell you that I support the Socrates program with all my heart—with my very life."

A single shot rang out! Eddy Domingo slumped to the floor. Mayhem! Shouting . . . people running in all directions . . . TV cameras scanning the Garden, but at least one kept on the prostrate Domingo. Lights flooded the arena, but now Eddy was blocked from all view. He was surrounded by concerned men and women. Doctors were paged. Security forces began to work for some sort of order.

The announcer for the "Domingo Hour" asked that everyone be quiet and remain in place for a few moments, then turned from the microphone for an instant and, looking back to the crowd, tears filling his eyes, in a cracking voice said, "A doctor has just said Eddy Domingo has been shot through the heart! *He is dead!*"

For a short time it appeared that riots would erupt within Madison Square Garden. Then hysteria . . . and . . . finally . . . massive grief.

The cameras were shut down, and programming was stopped. There was nothing more to do. Eddy Domingo had been assassinated—murdered! Who could do such a thing? And why? Could the killer or killers be federal agents? Communists? Maybe hired killers? Was this meant to put an end to the Socrates Society? Rarely had there been so many weeping men, women, and children in one place. They were sobbing, "Dear God, he was such a man of God, a man of peace and love. He lived to help others. How could this happen? Why? Why? Why?"

At 9:09 P.M. EST, word of the Domingo murder flashed across the country. The news was hard to accept, especially in the Domingo home in Newport Beach. Louisa and the two children were staying with Eddy's parents, Roberto and Maria. All the family were watching the program on TV, and now, while shrieking and wailing in grief, they were descended upon by their loving neighbors.

In the Sacramento governor's mansion, the Gonzalez family had also been glued to the tube. When tragedy struck, the governor summoned an aide to arrange immediate transportation to Newport Beach.

At midnight, the governor of California arrived at the Domingo residence. Mike Gonzalez restored some order, and he and an aide began the agonizing task of making arrangements for the immediate future.

Rev. Eddy Domingo, the most popular evangelist in America, had no cathedral, no massive edifice of his own. His own church was modest and intimate. He'd devoted himself mostly to people needs and then to a worldwide flock. His close friend, the pastor of the Crystal Cathedral in Garden Grove, asked that burial services be held there.

On Sunday morning, July 8, the cathedral became the focal point of religious services in the country. More than thirty thousand people gathered outside the glass structure and watched the dignitaries walk somberly inside. Pres. R. Evans Lee led the government mourners. Cardinal Ocanti represented the Vatican. Governors and congressmen from nearly every state were there to pay respects. Diplomats from Europe, Asia, and Africa added to the celebrity list.

American flags were in evidence, but more prominently displayed were state flags of each of the fifty states, Puerto Rico, Guam, and the Virgin Islands.

When the flower-draped casket was being carried into the cathedral, the massive crowd began chanting, "Ed-dy, Ed-dy, Ed-dy!" Louisa and the two Domingo children were escorted by Governor Gonzalez and his wife, Paula.

Ministers, priests, and rabbis praised Domingo as a man of God and, more important, a man of the people in their eulogies.

Then, as the religious service was ending, Gov. Miguel Gonzalez stepped to the pulpit—he stood silently, to regain his composure, and then in a clarion voice began, "You've heard from the clergy and I believe they will help speed our fallen hero to a high place in heaven. I wish to pay tribute to my friend Eddy Domingo. Since we were children, I can't remember a time when we weren't the best of friends. So . . . you can imagine how much I'll miss him. Anyone touched by him, either by personal contact or through his ministry, will miss him tremendously. We will grieve because we no longer have his love and advice to guide us. Think, then, of the horrible chasm left in the

Domingo family, Louisa, Bobby, and Maria, his wife and children; Roberto and Maria, his father and mother. We must pour out our prayers and our love for them, because they have the first burden of surviving this hideous tragedy.

"If we remember Eddy Domingo—and we must remember him—it should be for the love and understanding he preached and practiced. Eddy gave his life to teach you and me how to share God's love with one another.

"Our hearts are full of sorrow today, but they should also be filled with gratitude, because we are ever so thankful that we've had this brilliant, young man of God with us during our present, trying times. Now, will you pray silently with me—pray that God receives Eddy Domingo as a new angel in his bosom of love . . . and pray that we, his family and friends, are able to bear his loss as we continue to learn from his messages of brotherly love."

A great quiet settled over the congregation and the crowd outside. Then there were loud sobs as men and women wept unashamedly.

Eddy Domingo was taken for his last ride on earth . . . and laid to rest while the words were intoned, "From the dust thou art—to the dust thou shalt return."

Chapter Ten

Even though coffee was being served, some of the presidential advisers and cabinet officers yawned and complained about the early hour. It was unusual for the president to call a meeting at 6:30 on Monday morning.

When President Lee walked into the room, it was obvious he'd slept little. His half-hearted, "Good mornin'," did little to raise the enthusiasm of his staff.

Addressing his chief of staff, Sherman Roberts, Lee said "Sherm, do you have a point of view regarding the Domingo murder?"

"Mr. President, at your direction last week, I've gotten together with the attorney general, Tim Fox of the FBI, and the mayor and the chief of police in New York City. The murder weapon has been recovered—it's a 30-06 rifle, and the assassin shot from one of the unused spotlight locations. Everything is under wraps, and for that reason the police have declined a mention of fingerprints. The assailant probably wore gloves, but still there were some recognizable prints. Three suspects are under surveillance. One is a captain of the NYPD. Another is a taxi driver. He's an immigrant who's only been in the country a few months—from Russia. A third print has not yet been identified—it could belong to a child or a woman. Quite small."

"Fox has seven agents working with the New York police, and he's prepared to do their bidding. Everyone understands the urgency and impact of this tragedy. Some of us met here Sunday morning to review things, talk strategy. I don't know if we accomplished anything. Everyone should speak for him- or herself. My own opinion is that Eddy Domingo is likely to be revered as a martyr for the Socrates cause."

The president looked at the man wearing a ring of stars on his shirt collar. "General Fargo, we want to avoid riots and massive demonstrations of civic unrest. What should we be doing?"

"Mr. President, I've been in touch with all the governors and National Guard units. The governors assured me they would call on the Guard at a moment's notice, and those units near potential hot spots are on alert. The areas under a microscope are New York, Boston, Philadelphia, Atlanta, Miami, Detroit, Chicago, and Los Angeles."

Theresa Merlin, attorney general, said, "Mr. President, I feel we need some urgent action on your part and that of Governors Gonzalez, Addams, and Hadley. If the four of you could appear together on both national television and radio, it might present a healing message."

"Sounds like a good idea—how soon could we get it on?"

"Why not today? You know all of them. Why not phone each one for an OK and we'll set it up for this evening?"

The president didn't need arm-twisting. The governors would speak from their capital offices while the president would speak from the Oval Office. The networks agreed on an interruption of their prime time schedules so the message could be delivered at 8:00 P.M. EDT and then replayed on the West Coast at 8:00 PDT.

The president opened his address to the nation by again offering sympathy to the Domingo family and Domingo's followers. Lee said it was his belief that Eddy

Domingo would wish to remind all people that he was a man of peace and he would wish everyone to remain calm in their grief.

Governor Addams spoke of Domingo's dedication to people everywhere and offered that "the only way we can truly honor this fallen man is in nonviolent ways."

Governor Hadley complained of the cowardly murder and proposed that every American pledge to do something special for a needy person, a relative or neighbor—"something generous and friendly, and we'll all call it a 'Domingo.'"

When cameras were switched to Sacramento, inserts showed the president as well as the two governors. Gov. Miguel Gonzalez stared into the cameras, momentarily silent. As his lips started to move, his smooth, expressive words tumbled out. "I share anguish and grief with so very many of you. You may know that our deceased friend was my *compadre* and I could tell you many private little stories about him. One thing is certain—Eddy Domingo wishes every one of us, friends and followers, even those of you who have never heard of him, to pay him a simple tribute. How would Eddy hope you would do that? If he were sitting with us this evening, I believe he'd ask you to take some quiet time and remember those suffering from anguish and disillusionment, from hunger and sickness. He'd ask you to be their friend . . . and so . . . be a loving friend of his.

"Eddy's wife, Louisa, is here with us. She has agreed to speak to you for a few moments."

The cameras focused on Louisa Domingo; her children, Bobby and Maria, were standing next to her. "I am not a public speaker, as you will soon know. However, I did ask Mike—I'm sorry, the governor—if I could thank all of you for your outpouring of sympathy. When he

106

graciously agreed, I also asked permission to speak to our Hispanic friends in our own language.

"I don't know how it feels to be a widow with two small children. All three of us, and also my parents and the parents of Eddy, are still numb over what happened. We do not have feelings of anger, but of a hurt that burns inside."

Her eyes glistened with tears, but she made no effort to wipe them away. "I've heard on newscasts that there is a danger of riots in some of our cities because of my husband's death. Please, I pray that will not happen! Eddy would surely be disappointed! Won't you pray with me each night for at least a week that peace and calm will settle over our cities? Pray that God will give everyone the strength to carry on and to lead a peaceful and productive life. Eddy preached the brotherly love of Christ, and as Jesus taught us, forgiveness is an important part of true love." Louisa Domingo then spoke in Spanish, asking for particular help from the Hispanics in changing the world for good. Finally, reverting back to English, she said, "Thank you, Mike, thank you, Mr. President—*gracias para todos.*"

The messages had their desired effect. Demonstrations were held in many cities, but all of them were peaceful. The largest was among Miami's Latin population, where a torchlight parade began at dusk in the Orange Bowl and lasted well past midnight.

An eerie quiet settled over much of America. The politicians on each side of the Socrates issue were prudent enough to avoid public statements. Churches and synagogues held special memorial services, and out of them grew the Eddy Domingo Relief Program. Food and clothing were provided to the needy in huge quantities. Plans were laid for privately funded Eddy Domingo housing projects in Los Angeles, Atlanta, and Miami.

Members of the federal government couldn't forget that the entire Western Hemisphere had a new martyr—a man who had actively supported the dissolution of the Union.

Chapter Eleven

August in Washington was normal—steamy hot. People on the streets were irritable, even hostile. Senator Shadow Johnson worked the crowds harder than ever. He spent most of his time in the city, since his main objective was to keep the heated tempers cooler than the thermometer. He was generally effective and won praise from leaders of both major political parties.

"Reverend Johnson," President Lee addressed him in an Oval Office meeting, "you've been instrumental in keeping down unrest in the city. Thank you for all your help. I know you have your finger on the pulse here. People listen to you with their minds and their hearts. We would surely appreciate your advice on the coming election. We certainly don't want the states to secede—I believe you are with us on that. How can we best get our message to the people?"

"Mr. Presi-dent, I agree with you that we don't want the states to se-cede, at least not all of them. In my judg-ment, it might be a good thing for some of them to leave the Union, because they are not full contributors to our society as a whole. You must agree that those with racist tendencies do not help the Union."

"Which states are you referring to, Reverend?"

"Without much effort, I can think of a few—like Montana, Idaho, and the Dakotas. Also Maine, Vermont, and

New Hampshire. None of them are strong civil rights states."

"Well, Reverend, do you have any suggestions regarding a format to beat back the Socrates program?"

"Socrates goes back to the time when nearly every country had slavery, especially among the Greeks. Wouldn't that be a good issue to hinge the program on? It wouldn't be entirely inaccurate to claim the confederation party policy favors slavery."

"Oh, I don't agree with that. They surely have high regards for the rights of individuals. I thought you knew Eddy Domingo—he was as powerful a proponent of personal rights as anyone I've ever known. Look, Reverend, if you have any thoughts we can use to develop a hold-the-fort campaign we'd like to hear them. My own opinion is that this is going to be a very tough fight."

The senator left the Oval Office after a few more minutes of conversation. Neither he nor the president felt they had accomplished anything.

On August 16, the FBI arrested three men and one woman charged as accessories in the murder of Rev. Eddy Domingo. No names were released on that day, but Sherman Roberts, presidential assistant, went in to see his boss armed with the known details. An ex–NYC police officer was the suspected culprit, but he had not yet been apprehended. All four persons arrested were aliens—the woman, Elena Marta Covado, lived in Brooklyn with three Hispanic men. She was employed by a firm of lobbyists in Manhattan.

One of the men arrested, Raul Jose Sanchez, a half brother to Covado, was apprehended at O'Hare Airport in Chicago, where he was employed as a baggage handler. Another, Hans Edward Mueller, was a computer programmer in the Pentagon. He was taken into custody at his home in Falls Church, Virginia. The fourth, Sadam Saddullah Hilali, a member of the Iraq UN delegation was arrested in Norfolk, Virginia. It was felt Hilali had directed the murder. Covado admitted a relationship with Hilali, and she speculated Hilali had accumulated nearly a million dollars to hire an assassin and also provide funds for the needs of their group after July Fourth. Covado could not provide the name of the assassin.

Three days later, on August 19, the body of ex–NYPD police lieutenant Davo Martins Burlynsky was discovered in the trunk of a rental car at the Norfolk airport. He had been shot twice in the head.

Now all names were released and the press had a field day inventing more intrigue than actually existed. Little else was heard or shown on radio or TV news programs. News flashes were issued each time a new morsel of information was uncovered by investigative reporters. Newspapers in major cities filled their pages with stories and pictures of Eddy Domingo and each of the known culprits.

Attorney General Theresa Merlin directed a massive investigative program that included every conceivable law enforcement agency. The fact that they all agreed to work together was due to her persuasive requests. The Domingo murder was a taint on the federal government—the crime was surely swinging public opinion in favor of the Socrates Society and its confederation movement.

Burlynsky had deposited $100,000 in the Chase Manhattan Bank on July 2. Payment had been made by Raul Sanchez on the last day of June. Burlynsky was to be paid another $100,000 by Sadam Hilali after the assassination. Hilali was charged with the murder of Burlynsky.

Melvin Thomas, a news reporter, in a copyrighted story claimed an interview with Elena Marta Covado in which Covado gave names of three prominent political figures who were targeted for assassination. Thomas refused to give the names—until Attorney General Merlin leaned on him. They were Pres. R. Evans Lee and Govs. Bradley Addams and Flint Hadley.

All four of the suspects were held without bail. There was no concrete evidence that an interview with Covado ever took place. Even so, the already-tight security of the president was strengthened and the two secession-minded governors were put under federal protection.

Under continued intense interrogation, Elena Covado implicated others. She gave the names of Peter Brandt, Mark Gest, and Billy Simpson. She described Simpson's two friends but could not remember their names. Hilali confirmed the names of Brandt, Gest, and Simpson and remembered the given names of Bobby and Max.

Within hours, the five Fresno neo-Nazis were arrested. The FBI swarmed in to search tirelessly for additional information. They were particularly interested in whether the Fresno group was affiliated with a German cell or other neo-Nazis in the United States.

* * *

The Labor Day weekend was coming up. It was generally conceded that both sides would pull out all stops to win support for their points of view. The man of small stature from Texas bought TV time to explain his ideas. His was a novel approach that was sure to appeal to many. He proposed the elimination of Congress and much of the federal bureaucracy: "The country could and should be run by the governors. They could meet with the president on a monthly or quarterly basis, and the president in turn would carry out the directives of the states. After all, in the original confederacy, the states were too weak to stand on their own, and that was the chief reason for a movement toward a new constitution and the emergence of the federal Union."

The federal government broke out their radio and TV ads, which were short, punchy, and very well done. The printed media program was more descriptive and usually filled a quarter to half a page.

The business community could see many problems from the Socrates group, and through the U.S. Chamber of Commerce they tailored special advertising bits to be included with their own commercials.

Cynthia Addams Spicer and her Kansas City staff had no elaborate advertising budget. Their task was to get each state house to sing from the same song sheet. All the representatives were sent back to their respective capital cities for ten days. When they returned, she hoped, a single theme could be hammered out that would have massive voter appeal.

By mid-September, Spicer was able to hold a news conference. In her preliminary statement, she announced there would be no national advertising, no attempt to tell voters in every area the identical story. "After all," she said, "our belief is that each state is a sovereign governing body and therefore each is responsible for its own citizens. We believe the national media, in its attempts to discredit us, will be beneficial in getting our story to the people on a broad base. It is our belief that the American people are more intelligent than the federalists dare believe. We expect them to vote their conscience in November, and it's our opinion, certainly my own opinion also, that the majority of voters will demand a dismantling of the federal government and put an end to its massive bureaucratic waste."

Cynthia stepped back from the podium momentarily to indicate she would take questions.

"Mrs. Spicer, as a leader of the Socrates Society, haven't you suggested to the various states that they zero in on the martyrdom of Eddy Domingo?"

"No; it's true we have discussed the memory of Reverend Domingo several times. Mrs. Louisa Domingo has kindly offered to support us, and she will coordinate her activities with Governor Gonzalez. Other than that, I know of no plans to even mention his previous support."

"Is there a particular reason you don't wish to capitalize on Domingo's name recognition?"

"Our movement is 'of the *people*'— plural. It is much more than the memory of one person. The Socrates Society is dedicated to the same principles that Eddy Domingo preached, and we believe his followers know that. Other people will be told how they will be better off under a confederation of states by people they know—their state and local representatives, small businesspersons, educators, and, of course, clergy."

"Mrs. Spicer, what do you expect to get out of this personally?"

"I've never practiced law with my husband. I plan to join his practice as soon as he and I return from vacation—about the end of November."

"What plans does your father have? After all, he's one of the founders of the secession movement."

"Governor Addams has not discussed his future plans with me. We speak frequently on the telephone, but that particular subject hasn't come up."

"Do you have a numbers projection on the voting? You are concentrating all your efforts on Socrates, aren't you?"

"The voting is nearly seven weeks away. Much can happen between now and then. The polls indicate we presently have a 10 percent lead on a total population basis. The most important numbers will be those on a state-by-state basis. There are some legal opinions that three-fourths of the states must vote 'confederation' for any state to legally secede despite the Court's ruling, which stated 'a majority of states.' I understand that new state-by-state polls will be out in a few days. Whatever they show, we expect they will change often before November 4. Our staff keeps in close contact with the state capitals, and they are quite confident—probably more confident than I am."

"Mrs. Spicer, do we detect a lack of optimism on your part?"

"Absolutely not! It's just that our wonderful group of people has so much enthusiasm and optimism that we have to remind them there is such a thing as opposition, I suspect that there is a divided opinion among the reporters here—you can't all be against us. I'd be interested in how you feel. Would you like to put your 'yea or nay' in a hat for us? I promise not to reveal the count, even if we are the winner." They laughed, some quite embarrassed.

"Mrs. Spicer, who constitutes the governing body of the Socrates Society? Do you have a boss or bosses . . . or . . . are you a loose cannon able to say and do as you please?"

Cynthia chuckled. "I hope that none of us is a loose cannon. If we were, whom would we be aiming at? Not the press, I hope. Anyway, that is a legitimate question. The governing body, as you identify it, is composed of the governors of the states favoring confederation. Our task is to furnish information requested by the governors. I serve as director and there is one member per state serving on the advisory staff. A few states have withdrawn their representative, but it's not accurate to say those still here are all a hundred percent for confederation. Anyway, no loose cannons—I don't believe there is even a pop gun."

"Mrs. Spicer, will you tell us which states have withdrawn their representatives and also which of the advisers are not supporters?"

"Only the individual governors would be privy to that information. We had thirty-seven persons in a meeting this morning, but some of the absentees were out for personal reasons. I have not been told by a single governor that he or she does not support us. On the other hand, I have been told by only a few that they do support us. Governors Addams, Hadley, and Gonzalez, for instance. When you asked for this news conference, I did suggest you could get much more specific information from the state houses."

"Aren't you being too modest, Mrs. Spicer? We know you authored most of the Socrates program. Many of the governors have stated publicly that they come to you on issues of law and for the suggested legislative program if confederation is approved."

"Goodness, you make it sound as if I'm the only person here. The Socrates program was the joint effort of many dedicated people. It was definitely not authored by any one individual. It's probably correct that many governors come to us for suggestions on future legislation. Even though they use my name, as the director, I hope they know the ideas come from our staff."

"Cynthia, do you keep at the issues until you've reached a consensus and then report back to the governing body?"

"Oh no. Rarely do we find unanimity on a thorny issue. We endeavor to offer several options—sometimes we might indicate the feelings of certain individuals as a matter of clarification. Our goal is government by the people, and as an advisory group we could not consider anything dictatorial."

"Mrs. Spicer, what is your relationship with President Lee?"

"I've not been privileged to meet the president personally. My father has always spoken highly of the president, and I know he is a close friend of Governor Hadley. My own opinion, for what it's worth, is that President Lee is an honest, decent, dedicated public servant. He is in an extremely difficult position because of all the things a president inherits, such as the deficit, entitlement programs, overloaded bureaucracy, and the inability to radically correct things. The legislative branch of the federal government has forced *us* to secession and confederation, not the executive branch."

"Well said, Mrs. Spicer. If the November vote is in your favor, do you have a job for Evans Lee?"

There was general laughter.

"If the president is interested in joining my husband's law firm with me, it could be considered."

"Cynthia, your organization has almost made a joke of abolishing so many federal positions and instituting a retraining program to gainfully employ the many hundreds of thousands of displaced workers. What sort of jobs will be available? Do you have a magic formula that will keep such a massive workforce from exploding the unemployment roles?"

"Gee, I hope none of us has been making jokes of such a serious issue. Our retraining program must fulfill the needs of the marketplace. Your question indicates we have not adequately explained how we are addressing those issues; I accept the criticism. Our largest task force is directing its talents toward economic issues. They recognize the urgent need to gainfully employ those persons made redundant by the elimination of federal jobs. A few days ago they said the option papers would be submitted to the governors the day after tomorrow."

"Will you tell us what will be given to the governors?"

"I haven't seen any of their preliminary notes—anyway, the governors will study the various options and release their recommendations in about a week. All of us are anxiously awaiting the program that is surely one of the important issues for the electorate to consider. Thank you for asking about it."

The news conference ended and each of the reporters paid his or her respects to Spicer.

Only moments after returning to her office, Cynthia Addams Spicer received a phone call from the president of the United States. "Cynthia, I watched you on CNN and I must tell you how much I admire you—even though you're trying to put me out of a job. You handle reporters better than anyone I know. Young lady, you and I should meet; please consider this an invitation to visit the White House and *me* the next time you're in the area."

"Thank you, Mr. President. I don't know what to say."

"Pay me a visit and have your say then. God bless."

The religious right was now divided. Those supporting federalism and the Union were better financed and used their treasury to sponsor network radio and television commercials. While their themes varied, some used scare tactics such as civil war, anarchy, slavery, mob violence, mob rule, and the total loss of civil rights.

Rev. James Meredith took over the Eddy Domingo evangelistic program. He did not inherit Domingo's charisma, but he was able to convey his own deep religious beliefs and his support for the confederation of states. Considerably older than Domingo, he had added appeal to senior citizens, while losing some of the youth groups. Meredith's voice ranged from a soft whisper to the explosion of a foghorn. The louder he spoke, the more his mop of white hair became disheveled. As his voice deepened, so did the lines on his face, and they became channels that carried away the rivulets of perspiration. His sermons were similar to those of Domingo as long as he kept to religious themes. Once he raised the Socrates issue, he thundered with eloquence.

Governor Hadley asked Mike Gonzalez if they shouldn't convene a meeting and include Meredith. Together Hadley and Gonzalez spoke to Brad Addams and within days plans were completed for a strategy session in New Orleans during the second week of October. Arrangements were under the direction of the Socrates Society. Cynthia immediately dispatched a staff to the Crescent City to make certain everything would be in order.

Three days of meetings were scheduled. It was not to be a miniconvention, but rather an open forum to exchange ideas and plan the continuation of a modern, reduced government after the plebiscite. Invitations were sent to all governors, and they were urged to include cabinet, staff, and advisory persons. The 535 members of the Senate and House of Representatives were included on the invitation list for the first time.

Trade organizations were welcomed as well as the battery of lobbyists and, of course, the media. Cautionary messages were sent out that there was no utopia and therefore practical ideas would be solicited from all sources.

On October 11, just three weeks before the people would decide the political future of the country, forty-three governors with their more than four hundred most capable people descended on New Orleans. Another four thousand politically interested men and women plus an equal number of union representatives, trade organization members, economists, professors, and federalists promised a lively three days. All sessions were to be televised, and there were hundreds of foreign media representatives in attendance, especially from European countries and the Asian nations of Japan, Korea, and Taiwan.

The opening plenary session was chaired by Gov. Bradley Addams. His welcoming remarks were brief—he reminded everyone that their opinions were valued and strongly encouraged participation of all attendees.

The first speaker, Gov. Flint Hadley, opened with complimentary remarks about his good friend Pres. Evans Lee and carried on, "President Lee is here in spirit, for aih know he cares for every single person in this land. Y'all should know that this movement, this desire for a confederation of states, this determination to eliminate the wasteful bureaucracy is because Evans Lee, or any president, has so little control over government. That's why we want a change. That's why we want our people to authorize a change that will eliminate the waste of Washington and put government in the hands of local people.

"Many things are to be decided here in these three days. Your voice will be heard. Some issues are monumental. We must set up arrangements so we continue to have a single market. We need to determine the makeup of the new confederation—are there to be changes from the original proposal? Before we leave here, we wish to decide on a tribunal or court to settle disputes that might arise. More than anything, our plans and procedures are to improve our lives rather than throw us into chaos.

"All of you have heard or seen the recent stories telling

us we should have another issue on the ballot—that of a monarchy."

There was hooting and laughter—and shouting of "*YES!*"

"Well, that could be considered at a later time. Now, we are obliged to follow the ruling of the U.S. Supreme Court, and that's what we are to plan during these days.

"We lost a powerful voice for confederation when Eddy Domingo was assassinated. We have gained a new spokesman in Rev. James Meredith. You will have an opportunity to meet him on a personal basis at any time—right now, let me introduce Jimmy Meredith to you. Jimmy will have only a few words this morning but he'll be our luncheon speaker tomorrow."

Meredith stepped to the podium amid light applause. Dressed in a medium gray suit, pale blue shirt, and red tie, he looked like a prosperous executive. An abundance of white hair highlighted his coffee-colored skin. "I am not a politician—I am a minister of the Gospel." The words came out simply and in a moderate voice. He stepped back from the microphone a moment, then literally charged forward. "My ministry has been in Southern California, and I was an assistant to Eddy Domingo." His voice grew in volume and then, as if it rumbled from his heels, he thundered, "Eddy was my savior! He picked me off the streets of Watts; he made me a human being who could and would care for every other human being on earth. Eddy didn't teach me the benefits of the Socrates Society and the confederation of states. I'm such an egotist that I believe I saw their values the moment I heard about them.

"I hope I have an opportunity to meet each of you personally. Like Governors Addams and Hadley, I hope to hear your opinions. I know we can make this land a better place if we work together." He looked at Governor Addams and asked for another minute. "I agree with you that it's unusual for a black preacher to say he has a personal friend who is a prominent governor—I can honestly say that. I've known Governor Gonzalez all my adult life. He helped me through school, as he helped many others. Mr. Mike, as many still call him, is the voice of today's people. He's not black; he isn't white—he's brown. Please listen to him! Ignore me and any of the others if you wish, but open your ears and your hearts when Mike Gonzalez speaks, because he will tell you and me how we can improve our lives and the lives of those around us."

Meredith received generous applause.

Governor Addams said, "We will hold Governor Gonzalez in the wings until later. You are now scheduled to divide into discussion groups. We will see you back in this hall for a buffet lunch, but please don't eat too much—we want you to stay awake all afternoon."

On a gigantic screen behind the stage, Lady Liberty in chains was projected. The beaming face of Eddy Domingo said, "Good morning; welcome to a new era in our lives." Then a shot—and the crumpled body of the evangelist. The screen went dark.

Chapter Twelve

Men and women used handkerchiefs to wipe tears from their eyes as they moved to their discussion groups. Many felt the enormity of their task—they were to supply ideas to convince millions of voters to authorize the dismantling of the federal Union. They were then to provide an operating program for eight states that would form a confederation to work in harmony and be responsive to the needs of the people. Even more was needed—their program must retire the massive debt of the present government and rebuild the infrastructure of decaying cities. When Cynthia Spicer and her staff pointed out those details, each representative recognized the awesome responsibility they were facing.

Randall Berger told the group that for the last half-century the federal government had made economic cripples of too many people who were fully capable of working. "Before we leave here on Wednesday evening, we must have presented a program to the governors that will have outlined practical and humanitarian ways of changing millions of people from welfare recipients to productive members of society—we are to provide our recommendations for the reemployment of displaced federal workers.

"On Tuesday," Berger told the group, "our task forces will be assigned new issues. Those are: foreign aid, emigration from nonconfederation countries, interstate immigration, and the very critical issue of customs regulations and tariffs. Those of you with special expertise on these issues will be assigned as group leaders.

"On Wednesday afternoon, there will be a news conference. Present plans are for all governors to attend, and the press will be able to question any one of them. If each of us were to be questioned as well, you can visualize the commotion. However, your own governor may wish you to be available for queries. If you have a point of view you'd like to express, you should be heard."

"Mrs. Spicer, I'm Holly Baker from Utah. If there are to be only eight states in the new confederation, what will happen to forty-two governors who will lose their jobs?"

There was nervous laughter as Cynthia stepped to the microphone. "There will also be 535 members of Congress out of a job—plus their staffs. Holly, I don't have a cut-and-dried answer for that. I am going to practice law with my husband. I presume most of the governors will resume the professions they left before entering politics. Should we consider a retraining program for politicians, governors included? I can think of some trite remarks that would only get me into trouble."

"You mean that many of them are not retrainable?" asked Baker. More laughter. "If we can retrain the military and those on welfare, it may be possible to reeducate some of the men and women who have been politicians," Baker said with a lilt in her voice.

Spicer added, "A good point. Since our opportunity of success depends on drastic reductions in bureaucracy, it might be wise to prepare a rehabilitation program for ex-politicos."

There was thunderous applause and when it settled down, the delegation began anew to prepare a revitalization program for Americans.

During the buffet lunch, delegates had an opportunity

to exchange many different points of view. The governors joined tables that had open space—they were anxious to hear . . . and to learn.

Dozens of Washington insiders, senators, House members, and two of the president's cabinet were in attendance. Senators from California, Michigan, Indiana, and Illinois offered strong pro-Union opinions. House members expressed their views, and they seemed divided on the Union versus confederation.

Dinner speakers were Govs. Emmett Brown of New York and Luke Edward Davis of Texas. Brown started, "I never thought I'd share a podium with the governor of Texas. Our states are too diverse, and our points of view have often been at the opposite ends of the pole. Why are we now singing the same tune? Why are we ignoring party labels? I am a mulatto with an eastern twang, and Governor Davis is a WASP with a southern drawl. We could spend hours telling you about the problems of our states, but in just a few minutes you will know that solutions for New Yorkers and Texans are very similar. Each of us has immigration problems—we share them especially with Florida, Arizona, and California. We share unemployment issues with everyone else. Education! Housing! Health care! Crime! Drugs! Welfare! Crumbling urban areas! You understand now, don't you? Nobody has unique problems. In our new era of government, one that is close to the people, we will have solutions—we will learn from each other—the new country/states will feed on the goodness and growth of each other.

"Without the yoke of Washington around our collective necks, we will breathe a new life into 260 million people. At least forty-two governors could lose their jobs. That was brought up this morning by our advisory group. Some of us heard their uproarious laughter and checked it out—that's how we know! They are planning a retraining program for politicians. What do you think of that?" Laughter and applause.

"Our people will have an opportunity to choose only the best among us to represent them. Those new governors—and many of them may well be unknown to us now—will have a marvelous opportunity to provide leadership under uniquely new circumstances. They will not be under the constant shadow of federal lawmakers. Instead, they will be tied very closely to people very close to their homes. We must get that point across to every voter—he or she will be represented by people in their area rather than by someone stashed away in Washington. A note of caution! We cannot promise utopia—we must retire a massive national debt, and that can only be done by hard work. And—you've heard it many times before—we must abolish welfare as an occupation, as a way of life."

Governor Brown received generous applause. Then he introduced Luke Edward Davis as the present governor of Texas and obviously a leading candidate for the American Heartland chief executive.

Luke Edward grinned and said, "Thank ya, Emmett. Aih don't believe aih could handle the new job. Aih'd have to learn to speak both Spanish and Yankee. Aih guess I could polish my Spanish all right, but how in the world could aih evah make the fahmers in Kansas or Nebrasky understan' me?"

People howled with glee.

"Let's be serious today. Emmett Brown told you that we share the same problems in Texas and New York—and, for that matter, in all the other states. So, you know we are in this together. Of course y'all know that! Do all the people who will go to the polls on November 4 know that? Our job is to inform them how beneficial our new form of government will be. They must know that they will be recipients of more opportunities, but that they must put forth more effort. Governor Brown said welfare is not an acceptable occupation. He's right—welfare will only be for those who are not able to work. Those who cannot work! Those who need special help!

"Did it frighten y'all to hear the New Yorker say that some of the new governors may be people not known to us now? It shouldn't, ya know. We want our new form of government to draw on the talents of the many clever, knowledgeable men and women who might professionally direct us to a new prosperity. We need people with new ideas who can help solve the issues of crime, of drugs, of decaying inner cities. If you know those innovative people, drag them into our fold.

"One of the good things about this meeting is that it includes a number of federal politicians. They have golden advice for us. I am also pleased that we have business, education, social, media, and professional people here to supply unique ideas. We must understand the human trait of expressing one's point of view and sometimes not listening to anyone else. Aih was quoted the other day—I'd said 'dictatorship was the best form of government.' I did say that, but in the same sentence I said the dictatorship should last no more than thirty days.

"When the confederation of states becomes our new form of government, I hope you will call on me. Aih will not be a candidate, as Emmett suggested. Aih'd much prefer to teach y'all how to speak more understandably. Between now and November 4, you and I have a grave obligation—we must tell all the people, even those in other countries, tell all the people about our plans to improve the lives of 260 million Americans."

Governor Addams thanked the speakers and exhorted

all to continue their fine efforts. He also told them a televised news conference was scheduled for noon on Wednesday.

Tuesday was dedicated to a distillation of ideas into a more formalized program. Delegates were under stress and many were irritable from the pressure. It was a perfect opportunity for Rev. James Meredith. At the luncheon, he said, "I feel very humble—the opportunity to speak to so many contemporary patriots is a privilege few others will ever have. In a meeting with foreign correspondents this morning, I learned of the high esteem in which you are held. But you and I have a formidable task before us if we are to preach godliness. Whose God? Does it make a difference? John B. Noss wrote so accurately that 'man's religions reflect his human need to feel at home in the universe and comfortable among his neighbors.' Do you have any idea how many religions are represented here? I can't be certain, but here are those made known to me today—besides Christianity and Judaism, they are Shintos, Hindus, Buddhists, Sikhists, Muslims and Zoroastrians. Know what? Their goals are all the same. Sooo—on this day, I am speaking to people of the world, to those of all religions. Permit me to remind you that your God will listen to your prayers and he will grant your petitions if you pray fervently." Meredith's voice now thundered from the deepest part of his chest cavity, "Lord, give us the grace to know God's will and . . . and the courage to do it!

"Please pray with me. Thank you, our God, for all your graces—for all the benefits you have given each of us. These days, in New Orleans, we are gathered to plan a new and more modern form of democratic government. We ask that you guide us in mind and spirit so that what we have to offer the American people will be good for them and, especially, pleasing to you."

In only a few words Meredith moved the people. He made them feel like brothers and sisters to all mankind.

Cynthia spoke to her father. An anticrime committee would like to present an idea to a group of governors. Governor Addams said, "Tell me who you'd like and I'll gather them up."

"Not any particular persons. Rather, they wish to review their thoughts with those of different points of view."

"Three o'clock in Room C; that OK?"

She smiled, then planted a kiss on the governor's cheek.

Cynthia introduced the members of the crime committee and then turned the meeting over to Brian Randolph, its chairman, from Oklahoma.

Brian told the governors, "We wish to share with you some thoughts and then sit with you to get your reactions.

"We believe we have a suggestion to profitably utilize some of the people being discharged from the military. We would recruit them into a volunteer group of people to form an anticrime unit, city-cleanup force, code-named something like City Rangers. They would be armed and work in tandem with all law enforcement agencies. They would be compensated at the level of their previous military pay scale.

"This force against crime and corruption would move methodically through a city, sanitizing neighborhoods, opening them up again to clean, safe living areas."

Those in the meeting quickly became involved in a critical problem-solving discussion. Most of them missed the cocktail party.

The dinner speaker was the Honorable Miguel Gonzalez, governor of California. He was introduced by Gov. Flint Hadley. The introduction was very brief. "If we didn't have a television audience, I'd just say, 'Our speaker for this evening is Mike Gonzalez.' For the benefit of our broader audience, I must tell you that the governor of California is one of the younger state chief executives. He is a mover and a shaker. He is an idea man who has proven an inspiration to many of us because of his political wisdom and his knowledge of human emotions. It's been my pleasure to work with Mike. I'm convinced he's one of the great humanitarians of our time. You tell me if you like him—Gov. Miguel Gonzalez."

Governor Gonzalez flashed his engaging smile as he stepped to the podium. He stood there, smiling and waving, until the applause died down. "*Compadres,* we are one people! I've seldom felt so certain of that! You and I are about to see a dream come true. We've been through the cane fields, and in just a few weeks we will get our reward. Between now and then, there is much work to do. You are hearing that from every corner. You know what has to be done. If anyone has a doubt, ask Cynthia Addams Spicer!"

A resounding cheer arose.

"I wish to take a few minutes to tell you what we must do—beginning November 5!"

It took nearly five minutes for the crowd to settle back down, because many got up from their seats and paraded around the auditorium.

"Our work will begin on the fifth of November because that's when the massive federal government starts to be dismantled. That's when government starts to be returned to the people. It will be a slow, delicate job—we want it that way because we insist it be done correctly."

"As the process begins, government will first be returned to the state houses. Only days after, a second consolidation will begin with the shrinking of governments still further into the '*Confederation of American*

States.'" More applause. "A tentative program will be available tomorrow afternoon—a road map prepared by the Socrates Society. It may not have answers to all our questions, but we will get suggested capitals of the new states and their territorial boundaries. We will get guidelines for operating government free of the federal Union. Many things are yet to be resolved. We will be given options on the delicate matters like the courts, the military, privatization of federal commercial operations, and suggestions on how to retire the debt we inherit.

"A transition team will be set up to handle this enormous task, and I'd like to suggest we give that job to the Socrates Society."

The ovation lasted three minutes.

"The Socrates group is responsible for the progress we've made so far. At the governors' meeting in the morning, I'll propose that for you.

"We will not live in isolation—our confederation of states will become more global than the present federal government. We will continue the use of the dollar as our joint currency, and because we will have a revitalized economy with a decreasing debt burden, our currency should again become the strongest in the world.

"My fellow Americans, you are privileged to be at the dawn of a new era in political and economic progress. Our people will be better-educated and healthier. Because of increased life expectancy, we have a committee working on how to lengthen our productive life—sort of 'rocking chair back to desk chair' or 'fishing pole back to shovel.' We know our seniors are happiest when they are occupied both mentally and physically.

"A thought—or suggestion—from you! Tell your governor or your state legislators how we can improve. Keep in mind that this is to be your government, one of the people, by the people, and for the people. Tell your neighbors to vote against confederation if they wish to continue freeloading, unfair representation and the evil pork-barrel projects. We welcome all others! Thank you . . . and . . . God bless."

The Hispanic governor received a standing ovation.

*　　*　　*

Wednesday morning activities centered around the noon news conference for the governors. Brad Addams would be spokesman, and Hadley, Gonzalez, Edwards, Brown, Bloom, Gardner, and Meredith would be up front to answer questions. Since many of the Socrates group wished to attend, they adjourned at 11:00 and filled seats reserved for them.

Governor Addams started, "Since the media has been present at all our sessions and many of them have been televised or on radio, we will have no formal announcement. We will go directly to your questions. Please give your name and affiliation and indicate if you wish your query addressed to a particular individual."

"Betty Halpert, CNN. Governor, will we be permitted to ask questions of your daughter?"

Addams looked at the other governors for advice. Getting none, he said, "Of course. Cynthia, would you please come up to the platform?"

Halpert asked, "Mrs. Spicer, do you have any comments on the remarks made by Governor Gonzalez last night?"

"No, Betty. Governor Gonzalez previously discussed with us the idea of a transition team, so that came as no surprise. As you know, he is very straightforward, and we don't have to guess what his words mean."

"Cynthia, you said you wished to join your husband in his law practice. Does this mean you've changed your mind?"

"Not at all. I hope not. Our work as a transition team will take only a few months. No change in plans for me."

"Marty Benton, *New York Times*. Who is the leader of this group? Is it one of the governors or a member of the secret Socrates Society?"

Addams chuckled. "Mr. Benton, I see you again failed your course in 'how to win friends.' If you wish to rephrase your question, we will give you an answer."

"My question is . . . who is the leader of this secession movement?"

Luke Edward Davis moved to one of the microphone stands. "Aih guess you got wax in yore ears agin, young man. Been on the dung heap, too, haven't ya? Aih'll give an answer to all the other folks heah, but aih do not expect you to unnerstan'." Then, in his polished English, he continued, "Ladies and gentlemen—and especially those of you in the respected media—you know we have deliberately not chosen a 'leader,' a 'top dawg' to my itty-bitty friend from New York. Those of you who have been monitoring the meetings of the advisory group know they suggested that be done immediately after the election. Several of the governors have compiled a list. We aren't ready to release names, and we don't know if it should be one man or woman or two or three."

Benton tried to get in another question, but Addams pointed to another reporter.

"Helen Reed, *Washington Post*. Have you been in touch with President Lee during this convention?"

Addams responded, "I haven't, Helen." He checked

with the others. "Apparently none of us has spoken to him."

"Do you plan to apprise him of decisions made here?"

Addams hesitated. "We have made no plans to phone the president as a group. It might be a good idea— one that we will consider."

"Tim Mafew, *Manchester Guardian*. Mrs. Spicer, I sense that your group is setting guidelines for the confederation to follow in foreign policy. Despite your announced plans to practice law, aren't you really setting yourself up to be a super secretary of state?"

"Mr. Mafew, the Socrates Society advisory group has been working on foreign policy guidelines. We are not developing 'consensus scenarios,' but we are preparing options on the issues assigned us. We feel our suggestions offer an opportunity for the confederation of states to adopt a rational program that will meet the needs of the American states and also help the *eight* states become full partners in the world of nations. It could be there will be eight secretaries of state—or only one. I'm not a candidate for any of those jobs."

"Ryan, NBC. Governor Addams, I'd like to go back to the question Marty Benton raised. Haven't you settled on having a single person who would be 'first among equals' to help keep the confederation in line?"

"I haven't considered it any more than England, France, Germany, and other European countries would give thought to one man or woman binding them, as you put it, to keep them in line. There will be time for action if the need for such an individual arises."

"Would you be in line for that job? Or your daughter?"

Addams grinned. "Not me." He turned to look at Cynthia—she shook her head negatively. "There's your answer."

"Leslie Meekers, Reuters. I wish to ask Governors Bloom and Gardner if they feel women have taken control of the Socrates Society and, for that matter, the whole confederation issue."

Gov. Diana Bloom responded, "I haven't counted noses. Are there more women in Socrates than men? Cynthia, is that correct?"

Cynthia Spicer said, "I'm not sure. We've never made gender an issue—can anyone help us on that?"

Randall Berger stood and said there were nearly three men to two women.

Bloom then continued, "As Cynthia said, the issue of gender has never come up in my presence. Helen?"

Helen Gardner smiled and then in her Maine accent said, "Most of the governors are men. At a convention, it's an advantage for us because we don't have to stand in line to use the rest rooms. My father was in politics all his life, and I have also been since graduating from law school. There were times I felt at a disadvantage as a woman. Not with this group of people, however. Here, it's not men versus women—rather, it's people versus problems."

"Mike Ready, CBS. Have you developed a stance regarding Social Security and trade deficits or trade surpluses?"

Governor Hadley replied, "We will absorb the Social Security program as it is now—for the present. There could be changes later, but not in the next few years. Aih expect the advisory committee to have some thoughts on all aspects of trade."

"Martin Benton, *New York Times*," he said slowly, clearly, and without his usual rudeness. "We haven't heard specifics about two important issues: the reduction or possible elimination of the military and also your planned action on our crime problems. What can you tell us about the plans you have?"

Randall Berger stepped to the microphone. "Yesterday afternoon, last evening, and this morning we've been working with the governors to hammer out our program. Brian Randolph of Oklahoma is chairman of that committee, and he can fill you in. Thank you for asking."

Randolph stepped to the microphone. He was nervous and had to get a glass of water to simmer down. "Wouldn't it be more appropriate for one of the governors to respond?"

Governor Hadley smiled at him and said, "Brian, y'all and your people did the work. Y'all know the proposals better than anyone."

Randolph started, "We felt there would be large numbers of men and women separated from the military. They would need jobs. We were looking for an effective way to use their talents. Mrs. Spicer previously assigned some of our committee to crime control, so . . . what we did was merge the two groups. Our proposal to the governors was to recruit men and women being separated from the military to form a uniformed, completely volunteer group to form an anticrime, city-cleanup force code-named City Rangers. They would be armed and work closely with current law enforcement agencies. These people would be compensated at the level of their previous military pay scale.

"We visualize the City Rangers moving through neighborhoods, cleaning out pockets of crime and corruption and making them safe for family life. Some discussions are still going on as to which city or cities to begin with."

"Ryan, NBC. Such a program sounds intriguing: very good. Would it include the rebuilding of city infrastructures?"

Governor Edwards responded, "We believe we have developed a wonderful idea in the City Rangers. It is our opinion that it should stand alone. The rebuilding of infrastructures is a critical item, as is the one of bridges and highways. Right now, we envision that as a separate program from recapturing cities from criminal elements. Not unexpectedly, Governor Brown is most anxious to start a City Rangers effort, and he expressed an opinion this morning that the rebuilding of New York City would follow closely behind the cleanup, clean-out of the pockets of crime and of the criminal element."

"Benton. Governor, that sounds almost too good to be true. What would you do with the criminal elements as you move them out of the neighborhoods?"

Governor Brown replied, "Some are illegal aliens and they will be deported—immediately. We may not have enough existing prison space for the others, so new facilities would have to be built. Meanwhile, rest assured, they will be incarcerated in well-guarded quarters. We intend to break the back of the drug scourge very quickly. No bunk, we now have an outlined program to dry up the source of problems, the drug cartels in our cities and states."

"Archer, *Star Ledger.* Two questions: Have you considered the legalization of drugs? Crime and criminals are a way of life in our country. If you deport or jail the current offenders, won't the mafia replace them?"

Brown continued, "We must and we will be alert. My friends, we've had enough! We are no longer going to let criminals control our cities. Legalizing drugs—not under consideration by me."

Addams announced, "We have time for one more question."

"Governor, a few days ago Mrs. Spicer suggested you

137

would release your economic plan. May we have details on that?"

Addams responded, "We have not cast the plan into stone. I can tell you that we expect to greatly expand foreign trade. Reducing governmental expenses is like cutting overhead costs in a manufacturing firm. Our companies will be more competitive in world markets than ever. We expect the needed extra workforce to absorb many of the displaced people. We wish each segment of the economy to become 'world-class'—and that will be possible because we'll have extra profits to support research, development, and plant modernization."

Someone yelled, "What is 'book' on the vote count—and how many states will vote for confederation?"

Governor Edison waved his arm from the sidelines. When he got to a microphone, he said, "Here are the latest Gallup poll estimates—popular vote—confederation, 58 percent; Union, 35 percent; undecided 7 percent. States for confederation—forty two. These figures are much higher than any of us previously estimated. I've not spoken to anyone quite so optimistic. At any rate, we are quite aware of the rules of Article V of the Constitution of the United States.

Addams said, "Thanks, Monty. Thank you, ladies and gentlemen. We appreciate your attendance, and we hope we can see you again on November 5—with big grins on our faces."

* * *

Governor Hadley was paged during lunch. Answering the phone, he heard: "Flint Hadley heah—can aih hep ya?"

"You could, if you would only call off that damn

referendum. Flint, I just heard your news conference. Have to hand it to you—a smooth job without being slick."

"Thanks, Evans. Aih wish you were on our side. Anyway, you may well be before the confederation is running smoothly. Do you believe the latest poll information?"

"I hope it's wrong by a wide margin! My own guess is that the numbers are too close for comfort. Our count shows things about as dismal for the Union. Flint, I'm curious about something—is Cynthia Spicer really going to leave government and practice law?"

"That's what she says. I haven't spoken to her about it personally. If we win, I hope we can encourage her to accept some responsible position."

"If you lose, I want her. Is your phone secure?"

"Aih feel comfortable that it is."

"If you lose, I want Spicer, you, and Mike Gonzalez for cabinet positions. Wish I had you all along, but those other two are real surprises. My friend, I'm not giving you a lot of bull. At every cabinet meeting you three are mentioned."

"Bet we're cussed and discussed."

"Discussed with admiration. We're not all ogres. Every one of us has been through the wringer. It's been a nightmarish experience, and I'll be glad when it's over. Of course I wish you only bad luck."

"Evans, aih regret this happened to you. If the voters turn us down, there will be a sense of joy that such a fine man is still at the helm."

"Flint, you surely expect us to hit you with everything we've got during the next two weeks. Some of our ads will compare confederation results with the breakup of the USSR and Yugoslavia. Our chances may look pretty sick, but we aren't dead yet."

"Evans, we've tried to keep everything clean and impersonal. Aih have not heard one single defamatory word used by any of our group. We all have great respect for the individuals—it's just the damn system that's out of control, like a runaway train. The bureaucracy is out of control, and on its present course, it will surely explode. We've compared what's happened in Russia and Yugoslavia and what could possibly happen here. We've scrutinized the reunification of Germany. Right now, our best minds are analyzing how to deal with Japan, Korea, and Taiwan. China merits special study."

"I wish you would have put those forces to work for the benefit of the Union on the day of my inauguration. We might have solved many of our problems."

"It's the system that's wrong, Evans. No mattah what happens on November 4, you and I should meet and review, chapter and verse, the background reasons for the need to change. Hey, man, this country is not only one that must alter its method of government to remain viable. We'll talk about that also."

"OK, my friend. Good to talk with you. Keep in touch."

The president of the United States left the Oval Office—he intended to take a much-needed nap. He made an emergency stop in the john to upchuck his lunch.

Martha Lee was concerned because her husband was so pallid. "May I have the doctor see you, Evans?"

He didn't answer but slumped to the floor. Martha screamed and help arrived immediately. "Get Dr. Weyland," she demanded.

R. Evans Lee had created his own crisis. He let the secession issue eat him up, and now his heart was sending out a warning sign. As the chief executive lay half-undressed, in his own bed, Weyland and two assistants worked with him. Yes, it was a minor heart seizure. He should be all right—with some rest! Lee was quickly wired

140

up to monitors, and a nurse was assigned to watch the machines as well as the patient.

Standing near the president's bed, Sherman Roberts said, "I'll tell the secretary of state [Forest Mathers] and the vice president [Ray Hartman]—nobody else! Let's keep the wraps on this."

Lee gave him a wan smile. "Sherm, my best friend is Flint Hadley and it's OK to tell him. If you tell him it's confidential, it won't go any further."

At seven o'clock, the doctors examined the patient and the printouts. The president was not in imminent danger . . . but . . . it was more serious than indigestion. He must have bed rest!

Before the doctors left his room, Lee called for Sherman Roberts. "This isn't something we have a right to conceal. Tell Hartman and Mathers immediately and set up a 'cabinet meeting' for tomorrow morning. After that, have General Weyland issue regular and appropriate medical bulletins."

Mrs. Lee asked, "Evans, is there anyone in particular you'd like us to call? Somebody, besides me, to help make you feel better?"

"You're a doll, Martha. Have Flint Hadley come see me."

"Mr. President, that man is the one of those that's caused you all this trouble!" Roberts went on, "He is the leader of the Socrates Society, that bunch of idiots that are doing their best to ruin the country. He should be the last man on earth you'd want to see."

"Yes, Sherman, I know how you feel, but he is one of today's true patriots. Martha, please call Flint and have him come up from New Orleans. Tell him to plan on staying here with us."

Hadley arrived at the White House midmorning and

was assigned to a bedroom before seeing the president. R. Evans Lee was feeling much better, though the nurse was still on duty and his vital signs were continually monitored. Martha Lee led the Florida governor in to see her husband after lunch.

Lee grinned broadly and said, "Thanks for coming, Flint. You old scoundrel, it's so good to see ya. Sit down and tell me a story."

The two devoted friends chatted for an hour about old times, the weather, and the discomforts of growing old. "We gotta put up with the aches and pains," said the president. "Better than the alternative." Hadley had been cautioned against bring up the referendum issue, so he kept the topics lighthearted.

The president was promised he could get out of bed for the evening meal. He insisted Governor Hadley be permitted to join him and Martha for dinner. The food was as light as the conversation—only the governor had a glass of wine. "What are your plans after November 4, Flint? Will you accept the governorship of South Atlantica?"

"Evans, aih've been told not to discuss politics with you."

"To hell with that! We are politicians and that's the most natural thing for us to talk about."

"OK, Mr. President. Aih've continued to answer that negatively. One of the Socrates committees spoke to me this week, and I agreed to serve as an adviser, if asked, and only for one yearh. Aih'd like time to write my memoirs—I feel it a duty to put on paper what's right with our system and then offer my own views on what's required to repair it. Aih have this malaise regarding most governments of today. Instead of doing what is right, doing what is correct, for their population, they eithah legislate in favor of special interests or cater to the social views which promise every individual an equal portion of government gifts. Evans, when we were growing up, our parents and teachers told us, 'God helps those who help themselves.' Instead, we are now often more concerned with those who refuse to help themselves. As Americans, we seem to have adopted the five and ah half billion people of the world—we wish them to think and live exactly as we do. Why? You and aih are students of history and we know there have been wars and plagues, feast and famine, as far back as records go. Why must we insist on making carbon copies of ourselves everywhere in the world? Aih believe in the corporal works of mercy, but certainly not involving ourselves where we are not wanted. Our form of government has not yet been proven to be perfect."

"I can't argue with you on what you've said so far."

"Evans, you and aih have built a reputation of being free traders. Today, aih'm a free trader with some reservations. I believe our markets should be open to everyone on a comparative basis. We should match trade policies with others, and if our trading partners have import restrictions and trade barriers, ours should be similar. American industry can and will then compete in a fair and equitable manner."

"What about the Third World countries? Don't you favor a beneficial relationship with them until they can compete in our 'dog-eat-dog' world?"

"Aih'm not so sure. Aih'd feel bettah about handling each one on an individual basis. My reasoning is influenced as much by an immigration policy as anything else. No city or state can continue to be inundated with immigrants who become wards of government as soon as they arrive. Why? Early immigrants came from whenever, and by their mood and manner they asked, *What can I do to help build this wonderful country?* I agree that a few newcomers still have that attitude, but I'll wager the percentage is very low. The reason? They see too many others living on the handouts of government or they feel the pressure of cheats and thieves. Good citizenship is no longer a virtue—maybe because crime is so attractive. Am aih being unduly pessimistic, Evans?"

"Probably not, but are we so much worse than our major partners?"

"Well, each has its own problems, aih know. Why should we feel responsible to solve all their issuhs? England has its share of political strife, yet their murder rate, on a percentage basis, is less than one-fifth of ours—seventeen and half percent, to be exact. Germany is plagued by the neo-Nazis. Should we help them rid their society of that vermin?

"Mr. President, aih support the humanitarian work we perform. But . . . why are we so often the only people concerned about the welfare of the Eastern Europeans or the Africans or the Asians? And . . . should we not give preferential care to our own people?"

"Flint, you make a strong argument, but there are often much bigger issues. We must weigh the cost of foreign aid versus the horrible cost of military action. It's much less expensive to pay for peace than for war. Don't you agree?"

"That's generally true, but in some areas we are out of whack. Israel gets nearly $4 billion a year, Egypt over $2 billion, and Turkey nearly three-quarters of a billion. See what I mean?"

"I know, friend. Will your new confederation of states resolve all that?"

"No, but the eight states will each understand they can no longer be 'Uncle Sugar,' and the trouble spots or troubled areas will understand they must appeal to eight

144

political units, any one of which might have problems equal to their own."

Martha Lee called a halt to discussions for the evening. "The president must get some rest." Governor Hadley agreed to stay on through lunch the next day. The two good friends embraced before Hadley retired to a guest room.

*   *   *

At the conclusion of meetings on Wednesday, the governors gathered for a finale dinner. Also included were Ben and Cynthia Spicer, Rev. Jimmy Meredith, Randall Berger, and Bob Smith. There were no speeches—however, many strategic questions were raised. Should a manifesto or declaration be released before the election? One that would list the deficiencies, the failures of present government, and specific proposals on how to correct them?

Governor Addams addressed his son-in-law. "Ben, what's your advice? Should we offer proposed solutions on how to fix every single problem?"

"Governor, we should recognize today, as the founding fathers did in 1776, that the present system is not working. Therefore, it must be changed. I have some concern about the correct plurality number, as do some of you. While it takes 75 percent to amend the Constitution, the Supreme Court has given us a new number and I'm willing to go on it.

"Yes, I believe we should present a document with our proposals on options to improve government. Not too many numbers, no charts to irritate people, but short statements on the key issues. All such material is available; it's what

145

we've been talking about for more than a year. It could be given to the printers within twenty-four hours. Randall could make a press release before the end of the day tomorrow." He looked at Berger, who was nodding affirmatively.

"OK, let's do it—any objections?"

There were none.

Rodney Farris said, "I'm still against all this, yet I'm prepared to go down to defeat. Should some plan be made for the eight to have a titular head or spokesman? What's the general thinking on that?"

Dean Justice replied, "We've had some discussions. Most of the ideas were favorable, but I don't recall sending anything to the Socrates people for study. Mrs. Spicer, what suggestions has your team on such an issue?"

"Our *Program for Advanced Government* brochure will be given to you within the hour. It lists several options—one is the appointment of a 'president' as titular head of the confederation. His or her power would be controlled by the eight governors, much the same as a commissioner of baseball formerly was. Another is the election of a Supreme Court justice, and that person would be given some political power as well as judicial authority."

Mike Gonzalez asked, "Cynthia, which of those do you personally favor?"

"Ben and I discussed that very thing this evening, and we believe the confederation would be better served by a president, a person of considerable stature who would be an advocate of the confederation on a worldwide basis."

Donna Jensen asked, "Did you and your husband put a name to that person?"

There were snickers, coughs, and other general noises of uncomfortable people.

Cynthia said, with a smile in her voice, "No

names—no prospective candidates. I do have a suggestion, however. While there are so many governors here with their aides, it might be a good time for you to talk over this whole issue. I do feel we will get a mandate on November 4 and—"

There was a great verbal roar of approval and then everyone in the dining room stood and applauded.

When order was restored, Mrs. Spicer finished her thought, "you may wish to move on that issue to facilitate the transition." There was more applause. The group was in a mellow mood, sensing a victory, even though success might still be elusive.

Brad Addams gained some semblance of quiet and asked for suggestions on how to proceed. Within minutes an agreement was made to let everyone present vote: 1, president; 2, triumvirate; or 3, court justice. Slips of paper were passed around and then collected. Addams asked if they wished a count made immediately or the ballots given to a committee.

Luke Edward Davis spoke loudly. "Let's hear the preference of this group right now. Aih'll help you do the counting."

Everyone didn't vote—there were two for triumvirate and three for a court justice. All the rest wished to have a president as a symbolic head of government. Addams suggested they think about who the candidates might be.

*   *   *

The greatest-ever media blitz exploded. Radio, television, newspapers, and magazines filled their time and pages with points of view about the referendum. The jobs of 535 congressmen and -women hung in balance, and each of them addressed the issues and his or her own opinions at every opportunity.

President Lee was recovering from his illness bout and scheduled two messages to the nation.

On Thursday, October 23, the president spoke to the nation from the Oval Office. He looked older and quite tired, but his voice was strong. "My friends, a good evening to you. In less than two weeks, the people of the United States will vote on whether this country will continue as a unified nation. You will decide whether the Union, the federal government, will continue to exist.

"We are all impressed with the many statesmen and -women, with the patriots and their different points of view, and the calls for change. My dear friends, there are a few simple facts you should know. Secession to make up a new confederation of states will not work—it has not worked in the past. The first constitution in our country called for virtually autonomous states, and it failed! That's correct—it failed! Our founding fathers learned that a strong executive and powerful central government were required if the United States was to survive as a cohesive entity. Those wise men who nurtured the birth of this country wrote a new Constitution in 1787. It went into effect on March 4, 1789, and it provided for amendments to keep it up-to-date. For more than two hundred years, our Constitution, our government, has provided growth and opportunity for the millions. The federal Union has provided stability, education, refuge, and the fulfillment of dreams. Our federal government is not without problems, but those that exist can be fixed. The central government of our country is the envy of the world. It is the most copied and the longest-lasting." The president went on for another forty minutes extolling the virtues of federalism and pointing out the dangers of a confederation of states.

In his wrap-up, Lee said, "I hope each voter will go to the polls, and when you're there, be mindful of what we have in comparison to any other country. Remember that only you can guarantee another two hundred years of American glory. Thank you—and good night."

The president got good marks from the analysts and the pollsters. His message was a strong incentive for members of the executive and legislative branches to work harder to save the country—and their own jobs.

Govs. Betty Davies, Montgomery Edison, and Luke Edward Davis provided a CNN panel on Sunday evening. The moderator promised to reserve twenty minutes for phone calls. Mrs. Spicer acted as co-moderator.

Governor Davis of Texas started. "Aih hope y'all heard President Lee the other evenin'. He's a wonderful man and aih agreed with some of the things he said. The president and I disagree on the issuh of the legislative branch of government. That's the 100 senators and the 435 members of the House of Representatives. Do aih think all of them are bad? Course not! They aren't all good, eithah. Anyway, this group of 535 people balloons up by the thousands when you add in their helpers—you know, the people who make dinner reservations, hail taxicabs, and take care of all those other little perks the bureaucrats live for. Whom do the members of Congress work for? They are supposed to work for you, their constituents, aren't they? Well, do they? Yah know, they cater a lot to the whims of lobbyists—aih don't object much to that if the lobbyist represents Americans or American professions or businesses. However, it doesn't seem right to me that one dollar in every five—that's 20 percent—is for either a foreign govah-ment or a foreign industry. See what I mean—see how our system is flawed. Our bureaucracy has grown so large and so powerful that they feel they can do no wrong!

"Do you know that every one of our fifty states is weighted down with the burden of interpreting, implementing, and policing the laws passed by the bureaucrats in Washington. In most states, that takes the largest number of employees—people who could continue working for you on more constructive endeavors. Yes, sir, yes, ma'am, we could—and we will reap much greater benefits from our tax dollars."

Gov. Betty Davies of Vermont followed. In sharp contrast to the drawl of Luke Edward, she flashed an engaging smile and then in a New England twang said, "Governor Davis gave you some idea of the problem of bureaucracy in Washington. You should know that the greatest number of bureaucrats are spread out over our entire country. They are your neighbors; they comprise the army of dedicated federal employees who spend their lives unraveling the mess made by the lawmakers on Capitol Hill. We will retrain them so that they may become highly productive contributors in a new society. Instead of sorting out the complicated chaos designed by Washington to confuse us, they will be stalwarts of an enlarged labor market that will help every one of us improve our standard of living.

"Most of you have known all your lives that the federal bureaucracy does not and cannot do anything that the states are not able to do for themselves. International affairs, you ask? A fair question. Our statesmen, even today, are drafted from the states and serve in the executive branch of government. They could continue to represent their new country/state. The big improvement would be policies that represent people in their own area. After more than two hundred years, we have learned that the needs of Arizona may not be exactly the same as those of New Jersey.

"In a confederation of eight megastates, you will be represented on a local basis at a cost we can afford—and still retire the massive $4 trillion debt the federalists have burdened us with. On November 5, we will begin the unraveling of the maze of departments and agencies that have lost their effectiveness because of the penchant for red tape. We will reinaugurate the 'home rule' policy that forced us to divorce ourselves from England in 1776! The system imposed on the colonists didn't work then, just as the current Union system doesn't work today. It's your opportunity for a new, free, democratic form of government which will be you, the people; by you, the people; and . . . yes, and for you, the people."

Gov. Montgomery Edison nodded to the camera eye, then said, "We don't only want to save money—we wish to improve our standard of living. To do that, we'll take the easy things first. We will improve the quality of our goods and services without raising the cost—the price you pay. Bridges and highways will be built where they are most needed, because you and your local leaders will make the decisions.

"It's always easier to talk about somebody else's problems, so I'll stay out of Illinois. Where do you suppose the most valuable real estate is in this country? Surely you'd have to admit New York City would rank high on the list. How about that portion of Manhattan just north of Central Park? Harlem? Or the Bronx? Extremely valuable land—both very close to midtown Manhattan—and parts of them just waiting to be rescued from inner-city devastations. Most of our cities with over half a million population have similar areas.

"Do you want a better postal system? Better services without spiraling costs? Of course you do. How about improved rail service? Extended rail service? More efficiently operated airports? We should privatize these services! Sell them to responsible investors who will operate them on a modern and highly competitive basis—for profit—and a massive savings to the governments.

"Let me leave you with this thought. The federal government today is overpopulated. Overpopulated by at least 50 percent—and the real tragedy is that bureaucracy feeds on itself. Bureaucracy has a gluttonous appetite for growth, and no matter what, it will continue to grow faster than we can imagine. My friends, our type of democracy is a better form of government than most; it just isn't as good as it could be. You and I owe to our children—and their children for the years to come—to put into place an improved method of governing. Better? Yes! Less costly to operate? Absolutely! We've tried the federal method for two hundred years—now, we should improve it. We will—yes—we will when we vote for confederation on November 4. Thank you."

Cynthia Spicer began accepting phone calls for any or all of the speakers. The first caller, a woman from the District of Columbia who was a receptionist in a government office, had a question for Governor Davies. "If you close down the federal government, what is to happen to me and all the others who are Civil Service employees?"

Gov. Betty Davies replied, "Several things are probable. You could be screened for further government employment. Since there will be many fewer openings than at present, you may not be selected. In that case, you could be entered into a retraining program. These yet unnamed classes will be for a specific time period, such as our present school terms. You would be paid for attendance time."

"Does that mean I could sign up for a six-month class and be paid, even if I didn't attend?"

"You would be paid only for the actual hours of attendance. I feel you are a devoted civil servant now and that you and every one of your coworkers will put in your full productive time. Are you on a seven-and-a-half-hour workday?"

The caller laughed. "Yeah, we're supposed to be there seven and a half hours. Much of the time, we sit around and talk. We don't have that much to do. But it's a wonderful place to work; we can go to the office to rest up."

A caller from San Diego for Governor Davis: "You plan to make further cuts in military installations, don't you? Where are all those people going to find jobs?"

Luke Edward almost grimaced. "Yes, we feel further cuts can be made in our military installations. Many of the servicemen and -women will be offered the training Governor Davies mentioned—and they will be compensated for their class time. As you know, many of our military personnel are highly educated, such as engineers, doctors, lawyers, and business specialists. We won't forget them; they will be given equal opportunities to brush up on their skills under the retraining program. The City Ranger force we've been talking about is to be recruited from experienced men and women being retired from military service. For a few years, at least, the Ranger needs may even exceed the reduction in military forces."

Caller from Chicago for Governor Edison: "I have been a postal worker for twelve tough years. What about my job security? I've worked my tail off and now you plan to sell the department out from under me."

"My friend, thank you for twelve tough years. When the postal system is moved into the private sector, there will be an urgent need for the diligent employee."

"Governor, what about some of my friends who have been goldbricks?"

"Training classes will be available, but I must tell you and all others that we aren't going to rebuild a new and vibrant America with people who do not want to work. We, the political leaders of the federal Union, made a serious mistake when we bloated payrolls for work that wasn't there. For more than sixty years we have coddled far too many strong, healthy men and women by placing them on welfare roles. People who have jobs must be productive. Persons losing jobs must be retrained for the future expansion of a greater civilization. Men and women who are capable of working should not be allowed to make welfare their chosen profession. Does that answer your question?"

"Yes, sir, it does. I'm all in favor of what you said. I hope you will be a part of the new confederation."

The next caller came on like gangbusters. "Luke Edward, this is Sen. Jimmy Collins. We elected ya to be governor of Texas, USA. We feel betrayed by your present political views. You surely know aih can't support your seditious program, and ya also know aih will do everything in my power to encourage Texans—and all Americans—to vote against confederation. What do ya think of that?"

"Jimmy, aih applaud you for voting your conscience and aih hope everyone else votes his or her personal choice when in the voting booth. Aih can understan' yore point of view. It was not easy for me to take a stand against the Union. Pres. Evans Lee is my friend, and aih hurt for him. But, Jimmy, things have changed dramatically. We cannot continue as we are—if we do, the history books will write our obituary as they have with ancient Greece and the Roman Empire. Y'all tell me if there is a better solution."

"I am Ambassador Saito with a question for any one of the panel. First, I must say I have been embarrassed by some of us . . . foreigners who dared to get involved in the internal affairs of the United States. My question is, what sort of relationship do you propose to have with foreign governments?"

The panelists all looked to Cynthia for a comment. She said, "It is probable that there will be a president to act as titular head of government. The new states must decide, individually or as a group, how they wish the embassy matters carried out. There will be substantial changes, I believe. We are now making plans for an early meeting to cover the international issues, provided we win, of course. Representatives from each state have already been given material—options, if you like—to study. I am not yet at liberty to mention them, but I won't believe any government will be disadvantaged. The Socrates Society has promoted fair and equitable treatment for everyone."

Saito continued, "Mrs. Spicer, two questions to you, please. Will you be part of the new government structure in any way? And, secondly, should I take your previous answer to mean there will be changes in the current free-trade stance of America?"

"Mr. Ambassador, I have agreed to serve as an adviser for up to a one-year period. I cannot give you an answer to your second question. Should voters approve confederation, the eight new states will be free to make independent decisions, if necessary."

"This is Mary Hatfield, president of Williamsburg Women's College, Mrs. Spicer. If you were elected or named president, wouldn't you stay in government? You have become a wonderful role model for women, and we believe you have done the Jeffersonian task for the Socrates Society. That alone should qualify you for any prestigious position in the new government."

"Thank you for the accolades, Mrs. Hatfield. I have carved out plans for my future, outside government. There

155

are many people capable of filling the presidential position."

"Can you name any, Cynthia?"

Spicer chuckled. "Of course, the three panelists here . . . and also Pres. Evans Lee. There are scores of good candidates."

"Mah name is Alice Walton and aih live in Tampa, Florida. The crime rate heah is intolerable. Drugs, murders, robberies, muggings—they get worse evah day. What are you going to do about that?"

Governor Edison was the first to answer. "Ms. Walton, your city is under siege, like many of the cities in my state. There are some days when we feel that crime has overtaken our lives. I do not believe that any government can eliminate the present crime plague on its own. We must begin our road to a crime-free society in the cradle. Family values must be restored, and they must be in place before a child enters school. Only then will our educational efforts be successful. Our children must be taught to respect the rights of others. They must learn the rules and regulations of a peaceful society and . . . and have the will to follow them. Of course that procedure, if you like, will take several generations, since so many of us now feel the rewards of crime are too great to pass up. The confederation recognizes the seriousness of things now . . . today. For that reason, we are proposing the City Rangers, an anticrime force made up of experienced former military people who will work to sanitize neighbors. They will clean out the drug pushers, confiscate weapons, and return those areas to safe havens."

Governor Davies said, "There is no easy solution to the crime problem. The use of illegal drugs is an important factor, but we'd have our heads in the sand if we felt drugs were the only cause. One of the better solutions we've come up with would be the City Rangers as auxiliary law enforcement teams. There would be a pilot program to regain control of areas, neighborhood by neighborhood. Many cities have already asked to be included. Recruiting volunteers from among discharged military veterans would offer employment to experienced men and women and provide immediate help in the restoration of civil peace. All the potential states in the confederation seem to favor such a program. I am repeating this because it seems to offer immediate help to our plagued society."

Governor Davis offered his opinion. "A copy of our proposal has already been sent to President Lee so that he may take immediate action, if he chooses."

Davies acknowledged that, saying, "Luke Edward is correct. We feel the solutions suggested in our study are so valuable that we are recommending they be implemented immediately by the federal government. We are confident of almost instant and beneficial results."

The next caller was from the White House. "This is Evans Lee—this afternoon, I received the City Ranger report from Randall Berger, and I have already scheduled a meeting at 7:30 tomorrow morning to study how quickly we can implement some of the recommendations. I wish to compliment Mr. Berger and Betty Davies, as well as Cynthia Spicer and her staff, for the innovative way they've tackled such a thorny problem. Of course we hope to preserve the Union. Nevertheless, we are pleased to receive constructive help from our opposition."

Governor Davies replied, "Thank you, Mr. President."

Questions continued for another seven minutes. With time running out, Cynthia Spicer urged every voter to register his or her opinion at the polls on Tuesday, November 4.

At dinner, after the telecast, Mrs. Davis asked, "Luke

157

Edward, how do you feel you did? Did you win anyone over or drive 'em to the other side?"

The Texas governor hunched his shoulders. "Aih'm not sure how to read the reaction. The pollsters will tell us in the morning. Ben, you have a feel on how we did?"

Ben Spicer said, "The crime question was most pertinent, and your answers were on target. The call from the president was the most significant point in the whole hour. He let the country know he was open to good ideas—that helps him. The good idea came from you, and that is a mark against the federal government. You must get that point across to the other governors! President Lee is such a decent man, so I hate to use anything against him, but . . . if you still want the confederation, it was handed to you tonight."

Everyone at the table took a deep breath. Monty Edison asked, "You really believe he gave us the 'smoking gun'?"

"You bet! Maybe not the gun, but certainly the ammunition. Move on it tonight. I'll wager the president's remark could add a couple of million votes."

Luke Edward Davis said, "Excuse me, folks. Aih'll have somethin' to eat sent to mah room." Turning to his wife, he added, "Honey, stay with these good people and collect any gems they have. Aih'm gonna make some phone calls right now!"

All felt they could be more productive to the cause if they began working the phones at once. Their dinner was concluded before it started—eight days before the referendum vote!

Chapter Thirteen

The Socrates staff began contacting each governor on Sunday night. Directions from Mrs. Spicer were to urge every one of them, even those not offering vigorous support, to use all their state and local media facilities to present the facts to the voters as each saw them. Media consultants were each sent the *Last Week* package outlining thoughts on how to reap the best support. The local TV affiliates of the networks, CNN, newspapers, and weeklies were prime targets.

Church groups were sent packages of *Hope for Tomorrow* and an invitation to phone the hot line with their questions. The evangelists from California, Arkansas, Louisiana, and Virginia all had spoken in favor of confederation, and a package of material outlining critical issues was sent each of them.

Of the 535 members of the House and Senate, 137 supported the breakup of the Union. Each received a Federal Express package covering issues they could speak about. The remaining 398 received a short list of pro and con-Union versus confederation effects, with an appeal to let voters state their points of view. When questioned about the wisdom of such an action, Ben Spicer had the opinion that this might be the best way to have so many members of Congress shoot themselves in the foot.

On Sunday evening, Pres. R. Evans Lee and members of his cabinet appeared on network television for forty-five minutes. Each extolled the benefits of the federal Union, covering domestic and foreign advantages. They also reviewed other governments and the horrible mess when their central governing body lost control. Finally the president spoke of the past glory of the United States of America and his dedication to solving present problems and pointing the country in the direction of a bright new future.

As soon as the telecast was completed the president and his cabinet moved to a small conference room. When he spoke, Evans Lee was more relaxed than anyone had seen him during the past year.

"Each of you is to immediately begin making plans for a transition to a new form of government. I hope it will be wasted effort, but my intuition tells me we will be defeated on Tuesday. We are not to be obstructionists—your devotion to your office and to the country must show through. If we win, we will adopt many of the Socrates Society ideas."

Sherman Roberts asked, "Mr. President, I still believe we will pull this thing out. If we do lose, what happens? Who will direct a transition to the new superstates?"

"I don't know, Sherm. Should we feel the ground slipping out from under us, I suppose I should phone Flint Hadley, Brad Addams, and Mike Gonzalez and invite them to come and present their takeover plans. Cynthia and Ben Spicer are the Socrates brains, and they should be included. It breaks my heart to be in this position, but I suppose it's our fate. Anyway, we know most of these people personally and can understand that they are patriots and their desire for good government is as strong and dedicated as our own."

"What the hell happens if some of them turn out to be

dictatorial ward-heeling political bosses who take unfair advantage of everybody?" asked the vice president.

"Ray, we've had our chance. I suppose we should go home and involve ourselves in local government to prevent any such destructive forces." The president went on, "Their platform, if that's what it's called, offers some fantastic benefits. Reduction in operating costs, being closer to the people, more concern for next-door neighbors than those in foreign countries—how can we beat that? I'd be much more concerned if the leaders were flaky zealots—from what I know of them, they are solid, conservative advocates of good government. We must offer our professional help, and if it's accepted, we must pitch in with all our vitality. We have as much at stake as anyone else, and if we are turned out to pasture, we want them, as our successors, to succeed. Can any of you disagree with that?"

It was a glum-looking group of men and women who said good night to the president. Sherman Roberts quipped, "Any last words, boss?"

"Pray—pray that God's will be done!"

Former president Clay Farrington and ex-senator and previous presidential candidate Herbert Fullman followed President Lee on television.

Senator Fullman began, "We are living in a momentous time for America and for the free world. We love our country and we love American ways. Many of you have served the country and its people in some way, and I know there must be apprehension about the changes that are being discussed. It's easy enough for us to take the attitude that our government has done well for us for two hundred years; then why change now?

"Times have changed and I believe that if Benjamin

Franklin, Thomas Jefferson, and the other authors of our breed from Great Britain could zoom back in a time capsule, they would favor the breakup of the federal Union and the formation of a government closely resembling the one proposed by the Socrates Society. The federal government has not been able to keep up with the needs of today. You and I have changed and we now demand more for our tax dollars. We expect our elected officials to be more responsive to our needs, and today's bureaucracy does not permit that. On Tuesday, I will vote for confederation. I hope you will join me.

"Now, it's my privilege to introduce to you our former president of the United States of America, the Honorable Clayton Farrington."

"Thank you, Herb Fullman. Friends, you've heard both sides of the federal-Union-versus-confederation debate for so long—now you hope the whole issue will be resolved one way or the other and you can get on with your life.

"It makes a serious difference which way you vote. Confederation offers a more workable government today! Federalism guarantees that things will continue as they have for more than a half-century . . . taxes increase . . . your living standards decreases . . . and you wonder why we treat foreign governments and people in foreign lands better than we are treated ourselves.

"You can make a difference by joining me, Senator Fullman, and millions of other Americans in voting for confederation. Bless you all—and good night."

*   *   *

Monday went well for the president. He had visits from Britain's prime minister in the morning and from

Japan's prime minister in the afternoon. They were friends and he was able to discuss the next day's referendum vote in a candid, off-the-cuff manner. Both foreign leaders were deeply concerned about future relations should the Union be dissolved, and Lee assured them that the country was not about to tumble into a destructive civil war.

Besides the foreign dignitaries, there were the usual phone calls and visits from cabinet members. At 6:30, the majority and minority whips of both the Senate and House visited the Oval Office. Their moods were sour and fearful, and each hoped the president could pull a rabbit out of the hat—do something—and yet they knew it would take a miracle. The president listened patiently to each of them, and when they finished venting their anxieties he calmly told them that the massive growth of bureaucracy was a virus that threatened all governments. "We should have been more aggressive in our cost-cutting programs. We should have listened more closely when the people were complaining about pork-barrel projects. Each new administration during the last thirty or forty years inaugurated a study on how to improve government and do it at reduced costs. We have file cabinets filled with wonderful ideas and workable solutions to costly problems. As lawmakers, we ignored nearly all of them. I know. I was in Congress for twenty-six years before moving here, and we ridiculed every presidential task force and when a completed package was given us, we buried it, with a great fear that it might have something of value inside. My friends, I love this country above everything else. If we lose tomorrow, I will be sadder than I am today, but I will know the new government will still be American. There are some brilliant men and women in the Socrates Society, and I trust they will bring about the reforms we failed to install. I asked my cabinet members last night to do everything possible to make a successful transition. I also asked them to serve government 'at home' if they were asked. If any of you serve in a local capacity, I know you will have much professionalism to offer. Please do not forget the many foolish mistakes we've made and remember that our opponents seem to be beating us because they continue reminding voters that true democracy really is a government by the people, of the people, and for the people. I hope I can see you back here on Wednesday morning and say, 'We had a hell of a scare—now let's govern as we were elected to do.' Think that will happen?"

No one spoke, but, instead, they shook their heads. The president had warm handshakes for each of them and an *abrazo* for his old Senate pal as they departed.

R. Evans Lee, president of the United States of America, leaned back in his chair and closed his eyes—not tight enough to keep the tears from trickling out. He thought, *Lord, give me the wisdom to know your will—and the courage to do it.*

Lee sat still, almost in a trance, for half an hour. When he came out of his reverie, he stood up, switched off the electronic controls on his desk, and walked briskly to the living quarters. Once inside, he yelled, "Hey, Martha, what's for dinner?"